High Priest on Union Station

EarthCent Ambassador Series:

Date Night on Union Station

Alien Night on Union Station

High Priest on Union Station

Spy Night on Union Station

Carnival on Union Station

Wanderers on Union Station

Vacation on Union Station

Guest Night on Union Station

Word Night on Union Station

Party Night on Union Station

Book Three of EarthCent Ambassador

High Priest on Union Station

One

"In conclusion, it is the view of Union Station Embassy that the growing acceptance of humanity on the regional galactic stage leaves us woefully understaffed to deal with the problems and opportunities that now present themselves on a daily basis, and I urgently request that EarthCent fund a new full-time position for a junior diplomat in our office and fill said position forthwith."

Kelly smiled to herself as she wrapped up her weekly report for EarthCent and mentally removed "forthwith" from the list of words that she had always wanted to say out loud if the opportunity ever presented itself. Her warning about the increasing demand on the embassy was entirely true, and she imagined they could find ample work for several new employees.

Donna, her best friend and the manager of EarthCent's embassy on Union Station, had already headed home for the weekend, so Kelly wasn't surprised when she heard somebody calling from the outer office, "Hello? Is there anybody there?"

"I'm in here," she sang out in return, rising from her display desk in preparation to greet the unseen visitor. Her mind flashed back to a pre-immersive spy movie she had watched with Joe a few weeks earlier, in which the spymaster had a cover job as the cultural attaché in one of the old national embassies. Uniformed soldiers, an elaborate system of iron gates and sliding doors, and a bespectacled receptionist who kept a loaded gun in the top drawer of her wooden desk protected the embassy. Kelly was doubtful of the historical accuracy.

An attractive young woman stuck her head in the doorway, giving Kelly a preview of thick dark hair and liquid black eyes. Even though she and Kelly could now see each other plainly, the girl still knocked, or rather, she said uncertainly, "Knock, knock?"

"Who's there?" Kelly responded, assuming she would either draw a laugh or get a new joke to try on her seven-year-old daughter, but the young woman took Kelly's reply seriously.

"I am Aisha Kapoor?" she replied, making her answer sound like a question.

"Kelly McAllister. I'm the ambassador," Kelly identified herself, and moving forward to shake hands. Aisha, who had finally built up the confidence to insinuate the rest of her body into the doorway, seemed to come to attention.

"Ambassador McAllister?" she replied, her voice going up an octave. "I'm so honored. I mean, I knew I would be meeting you eventually, well, quickly, of course. I mean, I always knew there was a chance that you would be the first person I would really meet on the station, but somehow I never thought..." she trailed off.

"Please, come right in," Kelly encouraged her, leading Aisha to the chair next to her display desk that was most often occupied by Donna during their daily brainstorming sessions. "I have to be getting home pretty soon since it's my turn to cook, but how can I help you?"

"Weren't you expecting me?" Aisha asked with sudden trepidation. In response to Kelly's blank look, she fished in her purse and drew out an official-looking document that bore a suspicious resemblance to a repurposed EarthCent inoculation certificate. "I have my transfer orders right here."

Completely in the dark, Kelly accepted the sheet of paper and read it out loud.

"Congratulations Aisha Kapoor. You have successfully completed your EarthCent diplomacy orientation. Proceed to Union Station and report to Ambassador Kelly McAllister forthwith."

"After I looked up that last word and found out what it meant, I threw my clothes in a bag and spent everything I had on a supercargo ticket for the first non-stop trader coming this way," Aisha said. She rummaged around further in her bag and finally extracted a handwritten receipt for the fare. "I've never left Earth before so I don't know the procedure, but I'm assuming EarthCent will reimburse me for travel expenses?"

Kelly felt an overwhelming wave of empathy for the exhausted young woman and her worthless receipt. Obviously, the EarthCent training course hadn't changed much since Kelly joined the diplomatic corps twenty-two years earlier. The instructors never mentioned anything about the pay or reimbursements for out-of-pocket expenses because there was little of the former and none of the latter.

"We'll see what we can do," Kelly offered generously and accepted the receipt. Hopefully, Donna would have enough in petty cash to advance their new employee some walking around money until her first paycheck, without making the girl feel like she was accepting charity. "I have to admit that your arrival has caught me by surprise, but it couldn't have come at a better time. In fact, I just filed my weekly report and requested that EarthCent send us help, uh, immediately."

"Your weekly report? Oh, I still can't believe this is real. I've listened to all of your declassified weekly reports, some of them multiple times. The instructors hold them up as the gold standard for consuls and ambassadors. You speak in such lovely, long sentences and use such interesting words. I've tried reading the transcripts out loud to myself, but I always run out of breath before the period!" Aisha cut herself off after this last observation, worried that the ambassador might interpret it the wrong way, but Kelly was still stuck on the first part of Aisha's revelation.

"You listened to my weekly reports in the EarthCent diplomatic training course?" Kelly tried for an instant to recall everything she had said in almost ten years of filing reports, more than five hundred altogether, and gave up. She couldn't even imagine what it made her sound like.

"You didn't know?" Aisha asked in wonder. "It's practically the whole course, or I should have said, your weekly reports are the whole practical part of the course. The rest of the training was a lot of alien etiquette stuff that most junior diplomats will never get a chance to use. I mean, there were some reports from other ambassadors and diplomats, mainly about wars and disasters, but none of them do a weekly summary like you. Even though I just got here, I feel like I've known Libby, Gryph and some of the friendly aliens for years," Aisha practically gushed. "I must have saved an entire village in a previous life to be so lucky in this one."

"You listened to my weekly—no wait, I said that already," Kelly caught herself. She felt a little like a boxer who had just taken a rapid combination of blows to the

4

head. "I didn't think anybody listened to my weekly reports, other than Libby, and the Stryx aren't officially part of EarthCent. And they play my reports as a good example?"

"Is this a test?" Aisha asked doubtfully. "How could you not know that your reports take up more than half of the diplomacy textbook? All of the students joke that you could buy your own space station with the royalties."

"LIIBBBYYYYYY!" Kelly exploded, fists clenched, staring fiercely at the ceiling.

"Welcome to Union Station, Miss Kapoor. I hope you had a pleasant trip," Libby's voice came over the office speakers. "And is anything the matter, Ambassador?"

"Weren't you listening?" Kelly demanded. "You know perfectly well what's the matter. Aisha says that EarthCent has been using my weekly reports in the textbook on diplomacy for years and nobody ever told me!"

"You know I've always thought highly of your reports," Libby replied calmly. "Of course, I don't have any control over how the humans run EarthCent, but I can't think of a better training tool."

"It's not that I'm not flattered, but it would have been polite for somebody to have mentioned it to me, even just once in passing," Kelly griped. "And I've never seen a centee in royalties!"

"Hmm," Libby replied neutrally, an affectation she had recently adopted. The Stryx librarian's speech patterns had become increasingly human over the last couple years, perhaps as a result of handling all of the scheduling calls for InstaSitter. "Let's just have a look at, oops, here it is."

Kelly's display desk lit up with a densely printed document that looked like an ancient microfiche before magnification. Libby panned the image and zoomed in at the top, which read, "End User License Agreement for Diplomatic Implants, Version 3.098T6kf." Next the focus panned dizzyingly towards the lower left, pages blurring by so quickly that Kelly grabbed the arms of her chair in reaction. Then a single paragraph, highlighted in red, snapped into focus.

All official correspondence and communications of EarthCent personnel become the sole property of EarthCent. This includes, but is not limited to, the weekly reports submitted by ~~Acting Consul Frank~~ ~~Consul Frank~~ ~~Acting Ambassador Frank~~ Ambassador McAllister of Union Station. Any use or rebroadcast of EarthCent diplomatic traffic without the express prior consent of EarthCent is strictly prohibited.

"I'm really beginning to hate the EULA," Kelly grumbled. "And I don't remember signing off on any version changes, either."

"The original EULA included a waiver allowing it to be modified by EarthCent at any time without further notification. It is, of course, always available on file if you should ever want to read it," Libby pointed out helpfully.

"Are you paying attention to all of this, Aisha?" Kelly asked her new recruit sourly.

"Libby? THE Libby? Am I allowed to talk to you too?" Aisha asked breathlessly.

"Of course, Miss Kapoor. I am available any time you have a question or just want to chat," Libby replied.

"It's like a dream," Aisha said solemnly. "I feel like I should pinch myself to see if I'm really sleeping."

"Oh, I'm being thoughtless," Kelly exclaimed, feeling a surge of guilt that she had let her own concerns interfere with helping the tired girl to settle in. "You must be exhausted, coming on your first trip off of Earth and in Zero-G travel. I'll bet you haven't slept in days."

"It really wasn't that bad," Aisha protested, though the very mention of sleep drew a reflexive yawn reaction from the tired young woman. "But if you can tell me how to find the dormitory, maybe I should lie down for a little while."

Dormitory? This really is the poor girl's first assignment, Kelly realized. Had she ever been that young and innocent?

"The, uh, we—it really is a small embassy," Kelly said defensively, hoping to let the new arrival down gently. "You'll be staying with my family for the time being, until you settle into work and find a place of your own."

"With you? With your family?" Aisha asked, her eyes going wide. "I couldn't intrude like that. I'm sure that whatever accommodations EarthCent provides for new employees will be more than enough for me. I'm not as helpless as I look."

"Well, the thing is…" Kelly started, but she hesitated to tell the girl the truth about EarthCent's lack of provision for employees. No, she couldn't risk disillusioning Aisha and seeing her quit the diplomatic service for private industry before experiencing the rewarding side of the job. "The thing is that I insist," Kelly concluded. "We have plenty of room, you can stay in the main, er, house, or in one of the, uh, cabins. My husband runs a sort of a space camp. It's much nicer than it sounds."

"Living with a family is the best way for humans to become acclimated to station life," Libby chipped in. "Think of it as part of your training."

"If the two of you say so, who am I to disagree," Aisha replied cautiously, this time making a question into a tentative statement. "And I guess I am pretty tired after all," she added, looking positively exhausted now that the thrill of meeting two of her diplomatic heroes had burned through her remaining supply of adrenaline.

"Let's get going then. Where's your bag?" Kelly asked.

"My bag!" Aisha exclaimed. "I'm sorry, but I'll have to go to the dormitory after all. A robot butler sent by EarthCent met me when the ship came in and said he was assigned to bring my things to my room. I wouldn't have found my way here so easily if he hadn't given me directions."

"A robot butler?" Kelly asked, a dark cloud of suspicion forming rapidly in her mind. "Did this robot have a name?"

"Jeeves," the girl replied. "That's how I knew he was a butler." Her eyes suddenly grew even larger and rounder in her head, and for an instant, she looked like a Hindi movie star in a love scene. "You don't mean that Jeeves was THE Jeeves. I was still so dizzy from leaving Zero-G that I didn't think. Oh, and I even insisted he take my last ten centees as a tip!"

"I think I know where Jeeves took your bag, and don't worry about him being offended by a tip." Kelly shook her head, marveling at how Jeeves must have pulled strings to get EarthCent to leave her out of the loop about the new employee, just for laughs.

The first Stryx to grow up with human children had developed into an unrepentant practical joker, and his pranks were becoming more complex with each new attempt. But how on earth had he reached inside of Kelly's head and pulled out "forthwith?" Wait, maybe she had discussed her word list with Dring and the two of them were in cahoots. Kelly couldn't help smiling to herself.

Cahoots was another word she was just waiting for a chance to use in conversation.

"It's all very confusing," Aisha admitted softly, as Kelly led her back through the main office and out into the corridor. "Three months ago I was barely aware that EarthCent existed, and now I have an internship in one of the most prestigious embassies."

"Were you recruited out of university?" Kelly asked. "I was only twenty years old when EarthCent contacted me out of the blue and offered me the job. You look a bit younger than that to me."

Aisha's olive complexion grew a little darker, and she replied so quietly that Kelly had to strain to hear. "No, I never attended university. I was recruited after I took the entry exam for the new textile factory, or at least, I think that might have triggered the offer."

"Well, your family must be very proud of you," Kelly said, hoping to learn something about her new houseguest before introducing the girl at home.

"My family didn't really approve." Aisha spoke so low that Kelly had to rely on her implant for amplification. "But I told them I would take responsibility for my own dowry, so my younger sisters were all on my side. My parents are very traditional, but they don't have much money, and with a house full of daughters urging them to let me go, they gave in."

"How old are you, Aisha?" Kelly asked, suddenly wondering if EarthCent had gone into the foster parenting business.

"I am nineteen," the girl replied in a more normal tone of voice. "I know. You are going to say that a girl my age shouldn't need permission from her parents to take a job, but that's the way we were raised. If I had simply run away from home, my family would have disowned me. I've seen it happen."

"Then I'm glad your parents came around, and if you can't find a top-notch husband without a dowry when you're ready to get married, there's something wrong with the men on Union Station," Kelly told her.

"Thank you," Aisha replied with a catch in her voice, and Kelly was sure that the girl was blinking back tears from her eyes.

"So let me fill you in on our living situation," Kelly continued energetically as they entered the lift tube. "My husband rents one of the large bays on Union Station core for his business, which was originally a scrap yard. Then he got rid of most of the junk and ran a Raider/Trader barn for a year or two, but when the game programmers dropped all of the military nonsense, most of that business evaporated. These days it's sort of a hobby shipyard for locals who do their own mechanical work, plus a campground for space gypsies. Joe rents berths and tools to make repairs and modifications, and he converted a string of old gaming mock-ups into cabins, sort of an informal motel."

"A cabin sounds very nice," Aisha replied, trying to mask her disappointment. "Is it very expensive?"

"You'll be staying in the house with us," Kelly assured her, as the capsule door slid open. The two women emerged on the inner docking deck, a short walk from Mac's Bones. "We live in a converted ship, really just the crew quarters, and there's plenty of space. In fact, it feels kind of empty since Laurel got married and moved out after staying with us for almost six years. I'll put you in her old room to start, but like I said, there's plenty of room if you want to change."

The moment the two women entered Mac's Bones, they were assaulted by a pony-tailed whirlwind whose excitement prevented her from ever finishing a sentence as her thoughts raced ahead of her tongue.

"You're Aisha… Jeeves said… My doll started school… Metoo likes you… Beowulf is sleeping… I really don't need babysitters… Laurel's room?"

"Yes, yes and yes," Kelly replied to Dorothy, long accustomed to her daughter's hyperkinetic outbursts. "Aisha, this is my daughter Dorothy and her friend Metoo."

"I'm very pleased to meet you," Aisha responded in her best diplomatic manner.

"It is an honor to welcome a new EarthCent employee," Metoo replied. Although the little Stryx still followed Dorothy around like a puppy when his schedule allowed, his interactions with adults now reflected a maturity that Kelly suspected her daughter might never achieve.

"Come!" Dorothy commanded, taking hold of Aisha's hand. "Jeeves put your bag in Laurel's old room. And he paid me ten centees to show you where it is," she added, proudly displaying the coin.

Two

Joe quickened his pace as the morning tour of Mac's Bones took him past the abomination of a spaceship that Crick had the gall to refer to as a yacht. Unfortunately, Crick's dog barked and ran out to greet him, tangling herself in his legs and bringing Joe to a halt. If it hadn't been for Borgia, the maniacally friendly Golden Retriever who attempted to merge with every humanoid she met, the owner of Mac's Bones could have avoided some of the worst trades he'd made in years.

Few of the space gypsies and assorted vagabond families who camped out in Mac's Bones while making overdue repairs to their ships were flush with cash, but Joe knew that Shaun Crick would have resisted paying for a life preserver even if he was drowning in Stryx creds. Worse yet, the man hated to give fair value in trade. But the dog had already flopped on her back on top of Joe's shoes and was looking at him expectantly, so he crouched and rubbed her belly while waiting for the inevitable encounter.

"Morning, Joe," Mary called, having come out to investigate the dog's euphoric barking. "My hubby just went out looking for you. Said he had some business that would put a real smile on your face."

"Morning, Mary," Joe replied, wondering as he did every morning how a man like Shaun had ever landed a woman like Mary. Nearly eight years after his own marriage, Joe was beginning to realize that he had never understood women. He just hadn't been aware of the deficit when he was single.

A boy with carrot-colored hair came tumbling down the ladder, landing miraculously on his feet, and Borgia popped back onto her legs to run over and plant her forepaws on his thin shoulders. The two rubbed noses like Eskimos, and if Kevin had a tail, it would have been wagging in time with the dog's.

"Is Dorothy going to school today, sir?" the boy asked Joe politely.

"Nope, it's Saturday. But Aisha promised to give her dance lessons today, so don't be surprised if she ignores you," Joe replied.

Dorothy and Kevin were close to the same age, and people who saw them together always took them for twins. Joe and Kelly both liked Kevin and felt that his respectful manner and calm conduct was a good influence on Dorothy. Lately it seemed like the boy was spending more time in the McAllister's converted ice harvester than in his father's cobbled together pile of mismatched parts, many of which had belonged to Joe not too long before.

"I'll just run over and see then, sir," Kevin replied, but he waited for Joe's nod before he took off like a rocket, Borgia at his heels.

Joe turned back to Mary, preparing an excuse for having to leave without waiting for her husband, but she had produced a steaming cup of coffee from somewhere, along with a tray of pastry. The older Crick children had knocked together a sort of picnic table where the family took its meals, so Joe accepted his fate and sat down to wait for Shaun's return.

"He just has a thing about money," Mary said sympathetically, reading Joe's mind. "His own father got a hold of this ship somehow when Shaun's mother passed, and the two of them eked out a living as small traders on the fringes of Stryx space. Shaun would go months at a time without seeing another soul other than his dad, because the old man would never burn a gram of fuel if gravity wells and patience would get them there eventually. I think the main reason Shaun married me was for my cooking. His father raised him on dehydrated rations way past their 'use by' dates that they would scavenge from space dumps. Even with the exercise machines, he had bones like a bird when his father took sick and they practically crash-landed on Argus Eight, where my family worked as sharecroppers."

"I guess he must be doing something right to hold onto you and that passel of kids," Joe admitted grudgingly. "That's some life you lead, always on the move, no place to call home other than that sorry collection of scrap." As soon as he said it, Joe felt guilty about running down the only property the family owned, but Mary just nodded and smiled.

"It's a much nicer collection of scrap after two months of having new parts welded on, thanks to you," she replied calmly. "I only hope that you've gotten something of value in return."

"Of course he has!" her husband entered the discussion from ten steps away, his oversize ears pointed in their direction like a bat's. "Why, the Sharf circulation pump I traded him would cost thousands of creds new, and that's if you could find one."

Joe might have mentioned that the obsolete circulation pump needed a complete rebuild, the parts were no longer available and there was no demand for the working item, but he didn't want to make Mary feel bad. Instead, he rose from the bench and offered Shaun a perfunctory handshake.

"I heard you were looking for me," Joe said neutrally. "Everything going well with the overhaul?"

"Going well, the man asks," Shaun replied in amusement, directing his comments to his wife and the two older boys who had just emerged from the ship, still rubbing the sleep from their eyes. The Crick family also included three daughters, but the girls had left early in the morning to hunt for bargains on the Shuk deck. "It's going so well that it's finished! That's how well it's going."

Joe looked to Mary, who gave a disappointed smile in return. The Cricks would soon be moving along, and although their custom had certainly cost him more than he earned in return, he would miss Mary, the kids and their friendly dog.

"Well, that's great, Shaun. So where are you off to next?" he asked politely.

Shaun gave him an exaggerated wink in return and laid a finger along the side of his nose. "We're off to El Dorado, old boy. Going to fill the ship with gold, precious stones, and artifacts of a million years of culture. You've dealt with us square so I'm willing to let you in for a share. That's the best offer you're ever likely to hear in your life."

"I'm not a wealthy man," Joe replied cautiously. "I have to pay the Stryx rent on the hold every cycle, and these camp grounds and equipment rentals don't always cover the bill. If you're looking for somebody to finance a treasure hunt, I'm afraid it's not me."

"Oh, it's not money I'll be wanting from you," Shaun replied, rubbing his hand over the top of his balding head as he regarded Joe speculatively. "It's just a little favor from those fine connections of yours. A bit of a boost to get us where we're going."

"My fine connections?" Joe repeated in puzzlement. Then the meaning sank in and he corrected Shaun. "You mean my wife's connections, the Stryx. You know that they're very generous with Earth vessels when it comes to the tunnel network, so if you convince them that your, uh, treasure hunt is legitimate, they might waive the toll for a piece of the action."

"Well, there's just one thing about that," Shaun said, sounding a little less confident than usual. "The world we're visiting isn't exactly on the tunnel network, but it's not exactly off the tunnel network either. That is to say, the station librarian tells us the exit was closed some thousands of years ago."

"Sounds like the natives probably aren't interested in visitors," Joe replied, dismissing the subject from his mind. "Well, I have to get back to work, but I hope you all stop by and see us before you leave. I've got a new batch of beer that should be ready to try, and kids love a picnic."

"Hold on a minute," Shaun said, stepping in front of Joe and putting up a hand like an old-world traffic cop. "If I tell you about the gold rush of the century, no, the millennia, can I trust you not to spread it around?"

"You know that my wife is the ambassador, and I don't keep secrets from her," Joe answered, though the latter part wasn't entirely true.

"I know, I know," Shaun replied, and ruminated for a few seconds. "What if I told you that a wealthy old species has taken a vow of poverty and is giving away all of their stuff?"

"Are you serious?" Joe asked, mainly to delay while he examined the angles. For all of his sharp dealings, Shaun struck him as an honest man, and Joe didn't think Mary would stand by and let her husband tell blatant lies. "If that's really the case, half of the galaxy must already be on the way there, wherever there is."

"The way I understand it, there's something wrong with the local space that prevents jump ships from emerging anywhere near the alien's home world, and as I said before, the Stryx closed their tunnel exit." Shaun paused for a long moment and exchanged looks with his wife before continuing. "The thing is, my oldest girl, Becky, went through a religious phase in her early teens, and behind our backs she joined an alien order of nuns while we were on Setti Five. They gave her some sort of potion to drink that made her, well, sensitive, and sometimes she gets these visions, or callings, from the powers-that-be. Last night she received a calling that the time for the final distribution of treasure had arrived, and everybody was welcome to come and claim their share."

"How does she know where to go?" Joe asked, drawn into the story against his better judgment.

"The poor girl was given detailed instructions," Mary entered the conversation, drawing a concerned look from her husband, which she ignored. "But the instructions were obviously intended for people with much more advanced ships than ours. Something that could jump in as close as possible and make the remaining journey to the planet under its own propulsion system, not to mention landing or dispatching a shuttle, since the Kasilians dismantled their elevators a long time ago."

"I don't know," Joe said. "Maybe Gryph will be willing to help if it's legitimate, but somehow I doubt that relieving a doomsday cult of their possessions will meet the Stryx definition of fair play."

Shaun motioned his wife to hold her peace, and looked like he was suffering a thousand deaths as he considered the problem again from every side. But he must have known all along there was no way he could take advantage of the freak of chance that had given his daughter early notice of the greatest give-away in galactic history without the help of the Stryx, because he gave in with a sigh.

"The name of the world is Kasil. The station librarian sounded suspicious when we asked about it so maybe the Stryx already know what's going on, but I think the information should be worth something. I'm not asking for an exclusive franchise to the place, you know. Just a little help getting there and back so we can help these poor aliens prepare their souls for paradise."

"I hadn't realized you were a religious man, Shaun," Joe replied, allowing a hint of sarcasm to creep into his voice. "But it does sound like something the Stryx will be interested in if they aren't already aware of it. Why don't you send Becky by the house when she gets back so she and Kelly can talk it over with Gryph. In fact, I'll walk over now and invite Dring, since he knows more about all the old species than anybody on the station."

"I'll ping Becky and tell her to stop over as soon as she gets back," Mary answered for her husband. "The girls are stocking up on supplies, since who knows the next time we'll have a chance to get genuine Earth products in barter. I just hope there's some value to the craft jewelry they made for trading. Those girls put us to shame with their industry while we're traveling."

"Kelly mentioned that she introduced them to friends of hers in the Shuk, so I'm sure they're in good hands," Joe reassured her. "Thanks again for the coffee and danish, Mary. I must have let my belt out two notches since you started camping here."

Shaun insisted on escorting Joe part of the way to the scrap pile that cordoned off Dring's private docking area from the rest of Mac's Bones, expanding on his earlier explanation of the Kasilian situation.

"The order of nuns I told you about, they were dying out, see? Becky was acting funny those days, going off by herself in the hills to commune with nature or something, and she came across this old crone who had strayed too far from their convent and was struggling to get home. It turned out that these were the last nuns of the order left on Setti Five, and who knows if they still exist elsewhere? They had been hanging onto the religion since the Kasilians retreated to their home world and asked the Stryx to close the tunnel. I don't think that the nuns were Kasilians themselves, just local converts."

"So you're saying that maybe not as many people know about the give-away as the Kasilians who broadcast the invitation might have expected," Joe concluded.

"That's exactly my thought," Shaun replied approvingly. "For all we know, my daughter might be the only one in a position to actually act on it. And don't think I'm hoping to raid the planet of all its treasures," he protested, assuming an injured look in response to Joe's critical expression. "I just want to give my kids a better start in life than what I had. You know my wife is a saint to have ever accepted me."

The pair stopped at the entrance to the passage through the scrap pile that led to Dring's ship, and Joe spoke

19

seriously to Shaun. "I'll do what I can, but in the end, it's all up to the Stryx. If they agree to help you with this in any way, don't try to bargain with them. Just accept the terms, and understand that you're getting the break of a lifetime. They don't do things slowly, so by the end of the day you'll know one way or the other."

"That's all I'm asking," Shaun replied, sounding more like his brash self. "Give my best to the dragon."

Joe entered the tunnel that led through the remaining scrap mound from the days when Mac's Bones was a working junkyard, and emerged a few steps from Dring's gravity surfer. To call the shape-shifting vessel a "ship" hardly made sense in its current form. It looked more like the manicured botanical garden of a royal family or a leading university, and only the subtle shimmering of the transparent skin gave witness to the fact that the boundaries weren't natural.

Dring was working on one of his metal sculptures when Joe arrived, and not having brought a welding helmet with him, the owner of Mac's Bones quickly looked away from the white hot arc as the chubby dinosaur added a new bit to the current work in progress. Not wanting to interrupt, Joe waited until the hissing arc sound from the borrowed welding equipment cut out before speaking.

"Morning, Dring. Sculpture is coming along nicely," he ventured, though whether it was an abstract work of the greatest imagination or an exact representation of some creature that the Maker had come across in the course of his seemingly unlimited lifespan, Joe couldn't have guessed.

"Ah. Good morning, Joe. I hope you aren't regretting your generous offer of free scrap for my hobby. I begin to feel I'm taking advantage," Dring apologized, with an inclusive gesture at his rapidly growing sculpture garden. The dinosaur-like creature wore no protective equipment while welding, but he had an extra set of eyelids that functioned like welding helmet filters, and his skin seemed to be proof against all external hazards.

As an ancient shape-shifter with millions of years of experience, Dring had fine control over every molecule of his body, though it took him some minutes to carry out major transformations. His natural form was that of a small dragon, but the awkward wings and vocal chords that couldn't produce English speech led him to stick with his current manifestation during his extended stay on Union Station.

"You've barely dented the pile," Joe replied with a laugh, pointing at the mound of scrap. Not only was it true, but the rent that Dring happily paid over each month had become the most reliable source of income for Mac's Bones. While the hobby shipyard and camping business were always busy, payments were irregular and often took the form of barter, leaving Joe stretched at times to pay the lease on the hold. Profits from his micro-brewery business remained elusive. "Do you have a minute to talk about something?"

Catching the serious tone in the human's voice, Dring set aside his tools and waddled over to Joe. "Of course, Joe. I hope that nothing is wrong?"

"Not wrong exactly," Joe hesitated, unsure whether to repeat the whole back-story or just dive in with his question. He chose the latter course. "Have you ever come across a world named Kasil? I'm told they were quite an advanced species, but they adopted a sort of doomsday religion and withdrew from the galaxy back before humans started building stone walls."

"A very interesting case, the Kasilians," Dring replied thoughtfully. "Their leading scientist-turned-prophet foresaw the end of their home world, and rather than shifting the center of their civilization to one of their colonies, they chose to return home and prepare for the end. They were a race of pessimists, in decline for hundreds of thousands of years before that, and I seem to recall a whole genre of comedy that depended on a depressed Kasilian straight-man."

"Well, according to the parents of a teenage girl who joined one of their dying religious orders on Setti Five and has been experiencing visions ever since, the Kasilians are now convinced that the end is near and they want to give away all of their worldly possessions. I promised the girl's father I would have Kelly bring it up with the Stryx, and he's in a hurry to get there before the rest of the galaxy finds out and all of the good stuff is taken. As you're one of the galaxy's leading historians, I thought you might want to be the one to tell Kelly and the Stryx," Joe concluded.

"Thank you, Joe. I'll do that right away," Dring replied, displaying more energy than was his custom. "Would you like to come along?"

"I may not be a religious prophet, but I can see where this one is headed," Joe replied with a sigh. "I think I'll just start packing and getting the Nova ready for a trip."

Three

"You can't mean a planet full of people is choosing death!" Kelly exclaimed, looking from Dring to Jeeves and back again. Since it was Saturday and they were waiting for the Crick's eldest girl, the meeting was held in Kelly's living room rather than at the embassy. Sounds of traditional Hindu dance music wafted through the door from the recently completed front patio area, where Aisha was giving Dorothy and Kevin a beginner's lesson in classical Indian dancing. "If the Kasilians won't leave, can't you just move their world or something?"

"The Kasilians are an old and respected species," Dring explained patiently. "They were active participants in the galaxy's economy for millions of years, but around ten thousand years ago, they began abandoning their colonies and returning to their home world. Eventually they asked the Stryx to close their tunnel entrance, and now the Kasilians are forgotten by all but a handful of historians."

"It's not a question of technology," Jeeves reiterated. "The Kasilians forbade us from interfering. They look forward to the death of their world as a fulfillment of prophecy, their chance to become one with the multiverse. It sounds like the only reason they are coming out of seclusion at this point is to give away their worldly possessions before the end comes. We should learn more from the young woman with the visions when she arrives."

"Let me get this straight," Kelly stated. "We're holding this meeting because a teenage girl had a vision, this according to a third-hand account from my conspicuously absent husband who heard it from the girl's father? Shaun Crick would tell you that Earth is on fire if he thought you were dumb enough to give him a free ride there to help put it out."

"Kasilian dream visions are a historical fact," Dring informed Kelly. "It's not a communications system my own people ever employed, but it's a matter of record that non-Kasilian humanoids who participated in their faith and took certain drugs were susceptible."

"Oh, so there are drugs involved. That gives me a high degree of confidence in these visions," Kelly replied sarcastically. "And if you don't want to interfere, why are you even talking to me about it?"

"Perhaps Jeeves meant to say that we don't want to interfere directly," Libby hedged. Kelly glanced up at the ceiling in exasperation, shook her head and groaned.

"So while these poor deluded aliens are handing over their wealth and cultural heritage to every adventurer with cargo space who can follow a psychic, or should I say, psychedelic map, you want me to talk them into changing their minds?" Kelly demanded.

"You won't be alone," Jeeves told her. "Dring and I will accompany you, and I'm sure that your family would enjoy a chance to walk around on a real planet for a change."

"It's just for a week, a fact-finding mission to see how far their situation has deteriorated," Dring added. "No outsiders have set foot on Kasil for thousands of years. For all we know, there may be Kasilians who are open to other options."

Suddenly there was a loud yelp from outside, followed by a pause in the music. Kelly bounded to the door, expecting to see that Dorothy had accidentally tied herself into a pretzel while trying to imitate Aisha's graceful moves, but it was just that Beowulf had pinned Borgia under a giant paw and was taking his time about letting her up again. The young dog loved teasing the old war hound, literally running circles around him, but sometimes she became overconfident, and then Beowulf showed that he still had a few tricks left in the bag.

"Bad dog! Let her up," Dorothy scolded Beowulf, who easily outweighed all three of the dancers put together. Beowulf gave her a lazy smile and removed his paw from the smaller dog's rib cage. Borgia popped right back up, but rather than resuming her friendly harassment of the larger dog, she raced toward the entrance of Mac's Bones to greet the three Crick girls returning from their outing.

The Cricks were trailed by a Shuk mulebot, heavily laden with packages, so it was apparent that their trading had gone well. Becky broke away from her sisters and approached the ice harvester, while the two younger girls continued towards their cobbled-together ship. Borgia, scenting dog treats in the new supplies, chose to abandon Kevin and transfer her affections to the girls heading back to the Crick campsite.

"Mom pinged and said you wanted to see me," Becky said to Kelly with trepidation, as soon as she drew within easy speaking range. The eldest Crick girl paused to cast an odd look at her brother, who was standing on one leg with both of his arms outstretched and the palms held perpendicular to his forearms, seemingly trying to look back in her direction without turning his head. Like all children who passed extended periods in Zero-G, Kevin spent several hours a day on the exercise equipment that was designed to build muscle mass and promote bone density, and as a result, he was extremely flexible and well-coordinated. The boy had a much easier time following Aisha's movements than Dorothy, but living in close quarters with seven other family members had imbued him with the sensitivity not to embarrass Kelly's daughter by being too quick to learn.

"Thank you for coming, Becky. Please, come in," Kelly welcomed the girl, stepping back into the living room of the converted ice harvester. Becky was tall and thin, typical characteristics of children who had spent chunks of their childhood in small spaceships, and she moved with a combination of willowy grace and deliberateness, as if used to keeping track of the positions of her limbs.

"Is this about my calling?" Becky asked nervously, when she saw that Jeeves and Dring were also waiting.

"Yes," Kelly replied. "There's nothing to be worried about. Jeeves and Dring are here to see if there's something we can do to help the Kasilians. Libby and Gryph, the Stryx who run the station, are listening in as well. We're all worried that the situation on Kasil could turn into a riot of galactic proportions when word gets out. At the moment, you are our only source for this information."

"I'm not making it up!" Becky protested defensively. "I don't know what my parents told you, but if I could make the callings stop, I would."

"We believe you," Dring said soothingly. "And perhaps I can help you block these callings if you no longer wish to follow that path. But right now we just want to understand what you have seen, so we'll have a better idea how to act."

"I don't get the callings often," the girl explained, looking at the floor as she spoke. "About three times a year, they come like a dream while I'm sleeping, but I can tell the difference immediately and I remember everything when I wake up. Until this last calling, it was almost like watching immersive nature documentaries, with all sounds and smells, everything so real. I think they must have been showing the seasons somewhere because it was always about birds migrating, fish returning to rivers to spawn, the changing colors of vast forests."

"But there weren't any messages?" Kelly asked.

"There were always messages, but I didn't understand them," Becky confessed shyly, instantly gaining credibility with Kelly. "It's like when I was little and I would try to skip ahead and do the most advanced school lesson in the ship's library. I would understand all of the words, well, most of the words, but somehow, none of it made sense because I hadn't learned what came before. I think the callings described a system for living in harmony with the universe, and I kind of felt bad that I didn't get it."

"But this last message made sense?" Kelly pressed.

"Yes, the last calling was almost like a commercial," Becky explained. "Imagine if you wanted to sell everything you had, so you made a sort of an immersive catalog of all of the attractive items. But in this case, they just want to give everything away. The impression I got was that they wanted to be freed of material burdens before they rise to a new plane of existence."

"Your father is anxious to visit the Kasilians and help assume part of that material burden," Dring stated diplomatically, but the girl wasn't a fool, and she blushed in embarrassment. "The Stryx are willing to put us all through the tunnel together to check on the situation in person, precisely because we do believe your vision was accurate. And I'm sure the Kasilians could help you stop these callings with less risk of side effects than any other method. Are you willing to accompany us?"

"Of course," the girl replied simply. "I go where my family goes."

"Then scoot along home and tell them we'll be leaving after dinner," Jeeves spoke up for the first time since the girl had arrived. "Advise your father we will accompany your ship with the Nova. Gryph and the other Stryx will reopen the old tunnel exit, since that seems to be what the Kasilians want, but we will prevent any other ships from making use of it until we have a chance to assess the situation. I'm sure we all have many things to do, so I'll see you back here at 18:00 hours," he concluded, leading Kelly to reflect that the young Stryx had been developing his executive ability.

Becky merely nodded and headed off home, and Dring followed on her heels, probably to make use of the remaining time to prepare his gravity surfer for their absence. After Jeeves departed, Kelly put off her own thoughts of packing to enjoy a few minutes of watching Dorothy and Kevin trying to imitate their instructor's fluid movements. Shifting her gaze to Aisha brought her thoughts back to duty.

"Who is going to take care of the embassy while I'm gone?" Kelly asked the ceiling, knowing that Libby always had an ear open for her. "You know that Donna absolutely refuses to go to diplomatic dinners. She says she has too much respect for her digestive organs."

"Won't it be a good chance for your intern to get some high-level exposure to the other species?" Libby answered with a question of her own. "I know you're always worried that Aisha will leave EarthCent service to take a job with BlyChas, or even to work for the Hadads in the Shuk. Either choice would certainly mean a big increase in pay and free time for her. Letting her fill your ambassadorial shoes at a few diplomatic receptions might be the best way to keep her excited about EarthCent."

"But she's barely been here a month," Kelly objected. "And now that I think of it, the Drazen, Frunge and Dollnick ambassadors will all be attending the fundraiser for our shared ag deck tomorrow night. I was hoping to get them to talk, rather than throwing food at each other like usual."

"The Drazen, Frunge and Dollnicks have been throwing things at each other for thousands of years," Libby chided the EarthCent ambassador. "As long as Miss Kapoor has the sense to duck if something is cast in her direction, I can't see why there should be a problem. I'm sure that Donna bought tickets for both you and Joe, so tell Aisha to bring an escort if you're that worried."

"That's an idea," Kelly mused. "I'm pretty sure Donna told me that Blythe won't return from visiting InstaSitter franchises on the station network for another week yet, so I'll get Paul to accompany Aisha. He knows as much about the local aliens as anyone, and she should be comfortable with him since she sees him around the house."

"That's settled then," Libby said, rather smugly, Kelly thought. "You won't need your nose filters on Kasil, but Jeeves will have to reprogram your translation implants once you arrive. After thousands of years in isolation, the primary Kasilian language has probably changed quite a bit. And Gryph suggests that you all carry external voice boxes, as if this were a first contact mission."

"I haven't even seen a voice box since I left Earth," Kelly mused. "It functions like a reverse translation implant, right?"

"It's quite possible that the Kasilians no longer use implants, and they wouldn't be programmed for English in any case," Libby answered. "If you speak out loud, the voice box will wait for you to trigger it before translating, but you can also have it pick up the subvoc signal from your own implant and translate simultaneously."

"It's just for one week, right?" Kelly sought confirmation.

"Absolutely. Once you come back and report, we'll decide where to go from there. But if you see the chance to talk the Kasilians into evacuating or letting us act directly, don't hesitate to make a deal. As of this evening, you'll be officially detached from EarthCent service and functioning as a Stryx special ambassador for the duration of the trip," Libby told her.

"Is this going to cost me something?" Kelly inquired cautiously.

"Don't worry," Libby assured her. "Unlike EarthCent, the Stryx diplomatic service is fully funded."

Four

Paul good-naturedly took the evening off from working in his lab to escort Aisha to the ag deck fundraiser. As an advanced student at Union Station's Open University, he was researching practical methods for simulating gravity on vessels not large enough to do the job by spinning around their own axis. While the field had been exhaustively studied by gravity-loving spacefaring aliens for tens of millions of years, each species had its own preferences and notion of aesthetics for small ships.

Over the last month, Paul and Aisha had developed a nodding relationship based on thirty-second encounters in the kitchen and stolen glances in the living room, but both of them were shy. The two young adults also felt there wasn't enough time in the day to do half of the things they needed, so they had never spent any time really talking.

Although Blythe had been away traveling for nearly a month, Paul was so accustomed to her standing order for all of his free time when she wasn't busy herself, that he hadn't risked making any changes to his schedule while she was gone. Blythe often brought him along to serve as an unpaid employee of BlyChas Enterprises when she was on the station, and this evening, Paul wore a suit that she had given him for that very purpose.

"Is it alright, do you think?" Aisha asked timidly, appearing in the living room wearing a traditional sari of bright red, densely embroidered with fine needlework. "It's the only formal thing I own."

"You're beautiful," Paul stuttered when he found his tongue. Then his face turned the same shade of red as the fabric when he realized what he had said. "I mean, it's a terrific dress. You're going to make the other women jealous."

"It's actually my wedding sari," Aisha confessed. "My mother is a seamstress and she worked on it in her spare time for months. When I joined EarthCent and left my family home, I forfeited my dowry to my sisters, but my mother insisted I be allowed to take this sari."

"It's stunning," the young man repeated, feeling like he was seeing Aisha for the first time. After she arrived on the station, Kelly had sent Aisha to the Shuk to outfit herself with money that Donna had supplied from the embassy's petty cash, and the girl had come home with the lowest priced utilitarian coveralls she could find. The coveralls made her look like a station schoolgirl who worked part-time in a service industry job after she finished her lessons.

The EarthCent course and her month on Union Station had shown Aisha a different set of rules than her traditional upbringing, and as Kelly's stepson, Paul's status wasn't that of a complete stranger. The McAllisters had made her so comfortable in their home that she had almost forgotten that Paul was a man. Now she began to think that the sari might have been a mistake after all.

"We'd better get going, then," Aisha said in a rush, suddenly aware that with the rest of Kelly's family off to Kasil, she was alone in the ice harvester with Paul. How had she slept the night before with nothing but Dorothy's empty room between their compartments? How could she come back home with him after the fundraiser? She was beginning to panic just thinking about it, and her heart almost stopped beating in her chest when a warm body pressed against her side.

"Looks like Beowulf is a fan of your sari too," Paul said with a laugh, as the timely arrival of the normally supine canine broke the tension. "It must be the Huravian part of his heritage that appreciates it so much since Earth breeds can't see red."

The retired war dog shook his head at Paul, amazed that the human couldn't sense how uncomfortable the new member of Beowulf's pack felt. Sitting upright and lifting his head brought the giant dog's eyes to almost the same level as the girl's, and he gazed at her solemnly, trying to send the reassuring message that he would sleep on her rug tonight.

Aisha felt as if Shvan, the dog-mount who transported the Hindu god Bhairava to heaven, had magically arrived to protect her, if only from her own weakness for the handsome young man. She took a moment to scratch behind Beowulf's ears and over his eye sockets before asking Paul, "I assume you know where this event is taking place?"

"Sure. It used to be the Gem ag deck, but they let the lease expire. Jeeves told me they changed it into a park after they replaced the fresh fruit and vegetables in their diet with some sort of all-in-one nutrient drink, but it turned out that Gems aren't big fans of nature. No surprise there, I guess," he concluded with a wry smile.

The two young people walked to the nearest lift tube, where Paul spoke the instructions, "Humanoid-shared ag deck fundraiser, please." There was a slight sensation of acceleration as the lift began to move, but the path was largely along the station axis, only a few decks above the inner docking cylinder where Mac's Bones was located.

"I didn't know the elevators were so smart," Aisha admitted, anxious to get back on a more practical conversational footing. "I thought you needed to know exactly where you were going before getting on."

"You do need to know exactly where you're going," Paul replied in bewilderment. "Oh, you mean like having an address rather than an event or somebody's name, which is a good way to track people down, by the way. I've never asked exactly how it works, but my guess is that if the lift can't figure out where you want to go, it just kicks the request up to the next level, maybe a station maintenance bot. If the bot can't figure it out, the request goes up more levels until it gets to something with real artificial intelligence. If the AI can't figure out where you're trying to go, it would probably ask you for more details."

"I was never on an elevator, I mean a lift, before I was sixteen," Aisha told him, wondering why she was suddenly sharing details from her background that she had tried to keep hidden since accepting the EarthCent job offer. "I come from a small village in the countryside, and there were so many houses left empty after the Stryx opened Earth that there hasn't been much new construction in two generations. My grandparents thought that with all the people leaving to work in space, those who remained behind would have the opportunity to grow wealthy, but it didn't work out that way."

"Why not?" Paul asked, sensing a new bit of data for his analytical mind. "Wouldn't that have freed up a lot of land, so that the remaining farmers could grow more than they needed for their families and sell it on the market?"

"What market?" Aisha asked in reply. "The market left with the people who emigrated, and there was no possibility of exporting food before the orbital elevators were constructed, when I was around twelve. My grandparents and parents had plenty to eat and lots of room to themselves, but money was hard to come by."

The lift gave a sudden lurch as it changed directions again, throwing Aisha against Paul, who easily caught her with his gamer's reflexes.

"I've never been in a lift that did that before," Paul commented, as he set the flustered girl back on her feet. "Now you're going to think that the Stryx can't do any better than that first elevator you took at sixteen."

"I was sick after that elevator ride, though it might have been nerves," the girl admitted. "It was my chance to compete in the regional finals for classical dance, but I could barely keep my balance when I got off the elevator. After that, my parents stopped paying for dance lessons and I started learning to be a seamstress, like my mother."

"But you must have attended a good school," Paul said, though he didn't have the faintest notion what the education system in old India might be like. "Your English is perfect, and EarthCent recruits such a small number of candidates for the diplomatic corps."

"Teacher bots were free in India," Aisha told him. "The children in the bigger towns still attend real schools with human teachers, but in country villages, the language, math and science courses are taught by teacher bots, or tutor boxes, really. They're mass-produced on an orbital, and though nobody likes to admit it, the whole curriculum is programmed by the Stryx. My people are proud, but nobody could argue with the price."

"I wonder why it's taking so long to get there," Paul wondered out loud, then it struck him that Aisha might think he meant she was boring him. "I don't think I've ever been on a lift ride this long, and I've been from one end of the station to the other."

As if responding to his complaint, the door slid open, and the two humans were greeted with the strangest scene either had ever encountered. Rolling out before them was a lush carpet of grass, framed by sculptured hedges and rows of trees. Geometrical patterns of flowerbeds were distributed symmetrically around the white pebble paths, which followed the deck's curvature up into the ceiling. It was perfect and awful at the same time.

"What's wrong with it?" Aisha asked Paul. She grabbed his elbow, spooked by the view.

"I can't quite say, but it bothers my eyes," Paul replied. "There's the party, anyway. I never thought some folding tables with cheap plastic tablecloths would look better to me than a park, but they do."

As they approached the group of attendees, a Drazen male turned towards them and spoke. "Welcome, young humans. I believe I recognize the son of my ambassadorial colleague, and the lovely young lady must be the new EarthCent diplomat. I am Bork, the Drazen ambassador."

"Thank you for greeting us," Aisha replied, accepting the Drazen's warm handshake. "I am Aisha Kapoor, substituting for Ambassador McAllister tonight."

"Have you noticed anything strange about this place?" the Drazen asked with a twinkle in his eye.

"It bothers me somehow," Paul replied. "To tell you the truth, I don't think I would come here again myself, but of course, I didn't pay for the fundraiser tickets."

"Nobody would come here after a first visit," Bork informed them cheerfully. "The fundraiser isn't for the rent, it's to pay for tearing out all of these abominable plantings and replacing them with something natural."

"Are they plastic?" Aisha asked in wonder.

"Just as artificial," Bork replied in disgust. "There's a single blade of grass out there, repeated a few billion times. Millions of copies of the same flower, tens of thousands of the exact same bush, thousands of duplicates of that stupid tree. Those cheap Gems bought one of each and cloned them!"

"The Drazen is right, for a change," interrupted a tipsy Frunge, an empty glass in his hand. "I am Ambassador Czeros, a good friend to humans. So, where's the bottle?"

"I'm Aisha Kapoor, and this is Paul McAllister," Aisha replied to the Frunge ambassador's greeting. "I'm here in place of Ambassador McAllister, who is away for the week."

"I know, I know. No need to be so formal," the Frunge protested. "Didn't the Ambassador tell you she always brings wine to these things?"

"Aren't those your kids hiding in the shrubbery there?" Bork addressed the Frunge, pointing towards one of the sculpted hedges. The Drazen gave Aisha and Paul an exaggerated wink when the Frunge reflexively looked in the direction indicated by Bork.

"That's so funny," Czeros replied icily when he realized he'd been duped. "Your sense of humor must be greatly improved by drinking our irrigation runoff."

Bork's tentacle raised itself behind his head, a sure sign of bad temper in a Drazen, and Aisha had the sinking feeling that she had somehow precipitated her first diplomatic crisis. She reviewed her scanty EarthCent training in a fraction of a second, but all she could come up with were the scripted encounter games.

"May I make a suggestion, Ambassador Bork?" she asked the angry Drazen. "Ambassador Czeros is holding an empty glass, and I think he would be very grateful if you filled it for him."

Bork stared at the young human for a moment in shock, but then he broke into a wide smile. "Are we playing an EarthCent game, like the one Kelly used to put that little Stryx into a coma?"

Czeros broke into a gale of creaky laughter. "It is, it is. I believe she wants us to be friends. And here's where you're supposed to grab my glass, but I don't let go."

Bork obligingly took a hold of the base of the wine glass and the aliens pulled in opposite directions, causing the thin stem to break with sharp tinking sound. Czeros began to screech dramatically and Bork handed his piece of the glass to Aisha, saying, "But you told me to take it!"

Aisha's head swiveled back and forth in confusion, trying to remember if she had read about any similar behavior in Kelly's reports, but she came up with a blank. The two ambassadors were making such a racket that the others began gathering around, but all of them seemed to be smiling or glanding pleasant odors, so Aisha felt more foolish than nervous. Then she felt Paul's hand tugging on her bare upper arm.

"They're just playing," he told her. "Let's get something to eat before it's all gone. Nobody ever orders enough food for these events. You don't want to get stuck eating from a platter intended for some species that didn't show up, because even if it's not poisonous, it's not likely to be very good."

Aisha allowed herself to be led away to the buffet, which as Paul had warned, was already in the advanced stages of depletion. Providing finger food for a hundred or so attendees from a dozen or more species meant at most a tray or two of suitable comestibles for each humanoid type might be available at the start of the evening. Some species, such as the Drazens, were blessed with cast iron digestive systems that could handle, if not necessarily benefit from, anything they could bring themselves to swallow. Other species, humans included, took their lives in their hands when eating cross-species.

"Yuck," Aisha remarked, surveying the wreckage of what had been a mixed fruit platter. "If we had a bit of bread we could soak up the juice, but who knows how many hands have been in it."

"Human fruit always goes fast, it seems that most of the aliens can tolerate it," Paul told her. "It's the meat that they stay away from, especially cold-cuts, but you rarely get meat unless a lot of humans are expected. Oh, and I forgot that you don't eat meat anyway."

"It's alright, I can make something for us when we get home," Aisha replied. "Donna said that the fundraiser is only scheduled for an hour, and its sole purpose was to sell the high-priced tickets. There aren't any speeches or anything."

"Hey, they have a couple of bottles of beer left on ice," Paul said, eagerly grabbing a pair and reading the unfamiliar label. "Brewed and bottled on Union Station by the Earth Ale Consortium. Joe isn't going to be thrilled with the competition, but we may as well try it, just for the sake of research." He pushed down on the center of the pop-off cap on each bottle in turn and handed one of the open bottles to Aisha. She looked at it uncertainly.

"Oh, I didn't think," Paul continued. "Is it against your beliefs to drink alcohol?"

"No, not exactly," she ventured in reply. "But I never have before, and my mother taught me not to drink anything directly out of the bottle, at least in public."

"Here, use one of these," Paul responded, handing her a highly polished wine glass. "You can tell by the number of clean glasses that a couple of the early arrivals finished off all of the wine." Aisha continued to hesitate, so Paul took a sip from his own beer and gave her an encouraging smile. "It's really low alcohol content, Beowulf would turn his nose up at this stuff. But it's got a nice taste to it and I think you'll like it."

Aisha gave in and began filling the wine glass in her left hand from the bottle held in her right. But she had never poured beer before and didn't allow for the rapid frothing, so she ended up with a wet wrist and a few tablespoons of beer at the bottom of a glass full of foam.

"I think there's something wrong with this beer," she told Paul, looking critically at the glass.

"Here, let me try," Paul offered, just managing to stifle a laugh. He put down his own beer, took a fresh glass, and filled it carefully from Aisha's bottle. "You have to pour it on an angle, like this, and then it doesn't foam much. I can tell from the head that the brewers are using forced carbonization, rather than the natural method Joe says is better. Try this."

Aisha accepted the glass back from Paul and took a small sip, intending to say something polite, and then to surreptitiously leave the rest of the unfinished bottle on a table at the first opportunity. But the beer was a refreshing surprise and it didn't seem to contain the imminent danger she'd been led to expect.

"This is very good. Thank you," she said, rewarding Paul with a smile topped by a foamy moustache.

"You'll have to try Joe's homebrew sometime," Paul told her. Then he spotted somebody approaching over her shoulder and muttered, "Uh oh. Trouble headed this direction."

Aisha turned around and saw that the most beautiful woman she had ever witnessed in the flesh had exited the lift tube and was leisurely striding in their direction.

"Who is she," Aisha whispered back, wondering why they were suddenly speaking in undertones. Did the super woman have super hearing?

"That's Ambassador Atrea, a Vergallian. She came to one of our EarthCent picnics and Joe warned me to stay away from her. By the end of the evening, he had to warn her to stay away from me. The high-caste Vergallian women can do funny things with pheromones, and they go through men like a dog goes through bones."

Aisha's eyes went wide at Paul's story. The mental image of a stunning woman chasing men around the yard, chewing them up, and then burying their bodies in hastily dug graves, prevented her from preparing something to say to the ambassador.

"Well, well. What have we here?" Atrea drawled in a provocative tone, or at least, that's what the translation implants made of it.

"Ambassador Atrea," Paul replied first, since Aisha was momentarily tongue-tied. "May I introduce Aisha Kapoor, the newest addition to the EarthCent embassy?"

The Vergallian ambassador slowly looked Aisha up and down, as if she were committing every one of the girl's salient features to memory.

"It appears that I finally have some competition on this station," Atrea broke the silence languidly. "Have you any special talents I need to be aware of, or are you just a pretty young face in a gorgeous red dress."

"It's a sari, not a dress," Aisha replied, wondering where she found the courage to speak so sharply to an alien who oozed superiority from every pore. "And I dance, if that's any of your business."

"Ah, the tiger cub has teeth," the ambassador replied, displaying her own perfect ivories in a stunning smile. "And what is the tiger cub's escort doing this fine evening? Is he performing a duty from which he may be excused in time for a nightcap?"

Despite the acutely uncomfortable situation, Aisha couldn't help wondering what creature from the Vergallian worlds the translation implant had rendered as "tiger cub." She had been obsessed with the meanings and emotional tone of words since childhood, and she secretly suspected that her aptitude for linguistics was what had gotten her into EarthCent. Then she sensed Paul shifting uncomfortably at her side and mumbling something about somebody being warned, so she forced herself to focus.

"It just so happens that this 'tiger cub' and her escort are living together in the same den," Aisha declared with a brazenness that was all bluff, taking Paul's arm at the same time. "And speaking of home, it's about time we returned there. Paul?"

"Ta, ta," Atrea responded, adding an exaggerated wave before she turned away to look for fresh meat.

Aisha was trembling as she led Paul back to the lift tube, but she nodded polite greetings to everybody they passed, as the young man kept shaking his head as if he needed to clear his brain. When they entered the lift, it was

Aisha who spoke the destination, before self-consciously releasing Paul's arm and putting a little distance between them.

"Joe was right about that woman," Paul broke the silence ruefully. "Did you know that the Vergallians are actually the closest humanoid type to humans, and they planned on adding us to their empire back before the Stryx opened Earth?"

"I think she was perfectly awful," the girl replied, then found herself thrown into Paul's arms when the lift made a sudden lurch. The two were a little slower at disentangling themselves than they had been when the same thing happened on the trip out.

"I'll have to report this lift problem to Gryph," Paul said mechanically to cover for his embarrassment. "It never happened even once in the whole time I've been on the station, then twice in one night?"

"You should do that," Aisha agreed quickly, putting as much space between their warm bodies as possible.

The ride was mercifully short this time, and when they got back to the ice harvester, Aisha's idea of preparing a meal for the two of them went unmentioned.

"You know, I think I'll just return to my lab for a bit. It's early and I have a lot of work to do," Paul said apologetically before fleeing.

So Aisha prepared dinner for herself, and when she rose from her favorite reading chair a few hours later to go to bed, Beowulf got up and followed her into the room. There her self-appointed guardian sprawled out on the rug and immediately went back to sleep.

Five

Despite Shaun's protests that his ship was perfectly capable of landing safely on a planet with an atmosphere, Joe was skeptical. The original hull of the Leprechaun, which was of an obsolete alien manufacture, would have held up if Shaun hadn't nearly doubled the living space with additions over the years. The lack of aerodynamic engineering made no difference in the vacuum of space. But when it came to landing on a planet, even if the direct energy conversion webbing plastered over the modified hull successfully dissipated the reentry heat, the ship might prove uncontrollable or simply break apart under atmospheric stresses.

Jeeves agreed with Joe, so the Leprechaun was parked in orbit over Kasil and the Crick family transferred to the Nova. Kelly suspected that the real issue for Shaun was that he was losing all of the cargo space for treasures that his own ship offered, limiting his haul to what would fit in the now cramped interior of the tug. There were only two proper seats on the Nova's bridge, and Kelly gave hers up to Shaun as a consolation prize.

Planning ahead, Joe had covered the floor of the Nova's technical deck with a super-sized military surplus air assault mattress. The multi-layer inflatable device provided cushioning for soldiers making planetary insertions in cargo craft without proper seating, and doubled as an airbag should the landing turn into a crash. Dorothy and Kevin spent most of the descent attempting to jump up and down in the middle, trying to overcome the deceleration force. Kelly sat on the edge of the mattress with her eyes closed, hyperventilating into an air-sick bag, and she barely reacted when the propulsion system cut out and the ship stopped trembling.

"We're here!" Shaun declared, sliding down the ladder to the technical deck like an overeager schoolboy. "Joe couldn't get anybody on the comms and Jeeves said that the entire spectrum was quiet, so he's popped out for a quick look around to make sure it's safe."

"Everything is fine," Becky spoke confidently. "I just received a sort of waking vision and they're sending a welcoming delegation. I guess the historical records were right and we landed at the proper place for visitors."

"Jeeves says we can drop the ramp now," Metoo reported from above the mattress, where he had floated throughout the landing as a sort of a lifeguard for the amateur trampoline artists. "And he says to bring your voice boxes because Kasilians really have stopped using implants."

Shaun found the controls to open the main hatch, which also served as a ramp, and the adults and older children shouldered their pre-packed knapsacks before exiting onto the ancient concrete tarmac. Joe instructed the ship to secure itself, and then fell in at the back of the column headed by Shaun, which was hiking in the direction of the rising sun. Dorothy and Kevin ran ahead, shepherded by Metoo, and Kelly fell back to talk with Joe.

"Who put him in charge?" Joe asked sourly, lifting his chin in the direction of Crick family patriarch.

"He's just following Metoo like the rest of us," Kelly placated Joe. "If anybody is in charge, it's Jeeves, since he's the one who told Metoo where to herd the children. Don't be surprised if the Stryx talk to you directly over your implants because I gave them permission for the three of us."

"Thanks, but I'm surprised Jeeves didn't ask me for permission himself. He's such a stickler for the rules."

"You never resigned as the EarthCent military attaché, so you're officially my property," Kelly replied with a wicked grin, linking arms with her husband.

"They're coming! They're coming!" Dorothy and Kevin called as they scurried back to the column. Shaun came to halt just where the artificial surface gave way to dense vegetation, theatrically raising his hand for the others to do the same. Ignoring the hand signal, everybody continued on until they formed a little knot of humanity, plus one small shape-shifting dinosaur and a hovering, seven-year old Stryx.

The Kasilian welcoming delegation that emerged from the forest consisted of two wooden wagons, each drawn by a team of healthy looking quadrupeds. The draft animals didn't quite resemble any Joe had ever seen, despite his years of service on a number of technology ban worlds. The Kasilians themselves were only roughly humanoid, covered in a fine down and equipped with what first appeared to be a single long tentacle, but later proved to be a prehensile tail. The wagons were also accompanied by a few dog-like creatures, and Borgia raced forward, tail wagging, to sniff at them.

"Greetings, Lonely Ones and Follower," called the apparent leader of the delegation of three Kasilians. Now that they were drawing close, it occurred to Kelly that two of the aliens were teamsters. All three Kasilians wore floppy black hats, creating an impression of evil chefs, though Libby had assured the humans that Kasilian foodstuffs wouldn't cause them any harm worse than mild indigestion.

"Hello to you," Shaun called back, forgetting to trigger his voice box. "We're here to help relieve you of your material burdens."

"Shhh," Mary shushed her over-eager husband. "We accepted that Kelly would handle all of the first contact negotiations."

"It's not a first contact," Shaun protested. "These people have been around a lot longer than us, and it's our daughter who heard from them first. Besides, I don't think he understood me."

The wagons drew to a halt just before the grouping, and the native Kelly had identified as the leader descended by means of a short ladder fixed to the side of the contraption. Up close, the draft animals looked a little more natural, although they still didn't call to mind any Earthly associations, unless you included artistic conceptions of extinct mammals created from the fossil record.

Jeeves arrived back as the Kasilian leader was climbing down, and the Stryx took the opportunity to speak to the humans over their implants.

"I've analyzed enough conversations to update the translation equivalency tables, but don't be surprised if there are some misalignments. In short, their universal language has drifted quite a bit since they withdrew from the tunnel network, and the vocabulary reflects a shift to a low-technology agrarian society. Done. Your translation implants and voice boxes are updated. Don't forget to subvoc or you'll hear echoes of yourself speaking."

"Thank you for welcoming us," Kelly subvoced, nodding with satisfaction as her implant seamlessly screened out the translation generated by her voice box. "I'm Kelly McAllister, on temporary duty as ambassador for the Stryx. We came because this young woman, Becky Crick, received your calling. The Stryx are concerned about the possible unintended consequences of your coming out of isolation."

"I am pleased to meet you, Lonely Kelly, and you as well, Follower Becky. I am Kach, and I welcome all of you to Kasil. I have brought rapid transportation so you may reach Cathedral by nightfall," he said, indicating the wagons. "There you can meet with the appointed representatives of our people."

"Is the old tongue still understood here?" inquired Dring, who wasn't equipped with implants and was something of a linguist along with his other scholarly pursuits.

All of the Kasilians snapped to attention when Dring spoke, but it was Kach who bowed and answered, "You speak the Holy Language, Ancient One. Stupid ones like me do not understand many of the words, but our priests will speak with you easily. Please, come now. It is a long way to Cathedral."

The humans and Dring climbed up the short wooden ladders into the wagons, which were simple but finely constructed agricultural produce transports with benches added to the side boards. The adults ended up in one wagon while the six Crick kids and Dorothy clambered into the other. Kelly sighed and resolved to let Dorothy have her way as long as the wagons remained close to each other. She was about to ask Mary if Borgia would be able to keep up, when the "rapid transportation" started with a lurch, describing a slow circle to reenter the woods on the somewhat overgrown stone roadway. The draft animals moved at a pace that was probably no faster than she could walk.

"Could I ask you a few questions?" Kelly subvoced, hoping that Kach could hear her voicebox over the clatter of the hooves, wooden wheels on the stones, and the noise made by the wagon's rattling. She was glad to note that the wagon bodies rode high enough to allow her to see over the heads of the team and into the bed of the vehicle commandeered by the kids. Of course, with Metoo sticking to Dorothy and Jeeves floating about somewhere, there wasn't any cause to get worried.

"I will try to answer," Kach replied, and politely climbed off the driver's bench into the wagon bed to make conversation easier. But even as he sat down next to Kelly, he cautioned her, "I'm just a local farmer who happens to live near the old landing site, so don't expect too much of me. The district priest called on me this morning and asked if I could take two wagons to pick up visitors and bring you to Cathedral."

"Please forgive me if I give any offense, but the only information I have about your people is thousands of years old," Kelly began, noticing that Dring was listening with visible concentration, though she was unsure how much he could understand. "To begin with, other than the old concrete on the landing field, I haven't seen any signs of technology since we arrived. After millions of years as a space-faring species, did your people ban technology?"

Kach was slow to answer, perhaps he was puzzled, but Kelly couldn't read anything from his furry face. Finally he asked, "What does this word 'technology' mean?"

Kelly was stumped for a moment and thought about calling Jeeves through her implant to come and interpret, but then her pride took over and she decided to just take her time and explain. Besides, at the rate the wagon was traveling, there wasn't much motivation to hurry.

"Technology refers to the tools and machines you make, like the ship we arrived in, or even this wagon. I'll bet there was a time a few thousand years, sorry, make that a few million years ago, that your people had to invent the wheel. A wheel is a great example of technology," she concluded enthusiastically.

"Ah, I understand. So you have seen our technology since arriving. The wheel is a great example," Kach concurred.

"Yes, the wheel," Kelly echoed, wondering why the conversation was going in circles. "But after your people invented the wheel, they invented many other things, including ships like ours that flew to the stars, machines that could think and solve problems, methods of communicating over great distances."

"Oh, now I do understand. You're interested in the old machines, the things we gave up to become one with Kasil in her time of death and redemption. Our people did create much, how did you call it, technology, when we traveled among the stars. But now we all live in harmony with the land and those things are unneeded," the Kasilian replied.

"But technology isn't just about space travel," Kelly protested. "How about tools for growing food, and factories, and computers for keeping records of business transactions?"

"I'm afraid I don't understand some of the words you are using," Kach replied ruefully. "But I have seen and heard of the lives lived by aliens throughout the galaxy. Our priests make such visions available to those who wish to receive them every evening when our work day is done. The young and the old seem to enjoy them very much, but at my age, I prefer to stare into the void."

"You've mentioned your priests several times, and you called our destination a cathedral," Kelly replied, trying to not think about a life spent in contemplation of doom. "Are all of your people of one faith? Where I come from, there are dozens of religions with large numbers of believers."

"Again, your words are a little confusing," Kach reported. "Of course we all believe in the same Truth, it makes no sense to me that you could have dozens. Why, all but one of them would have to be false!"

"Oh," Kelly said, her lips making a perfect circle as she drew out the sound. So she was dealing with religious fanatics. I suppose that makes sense if they're bent on species suicide, she thought. But he seems so rational. "And the leaders of your faith are telling you to give up all of your worldly possessions because the end is nigh?" Kelly had to bite her tongue to keep from breaking out in laughter when she realized she had just removed "nigh" from her list of must-use words without even trying.

"Leaders?" Kach asked. "How can there be more than one leader of any one thing? There is only one High Priest, whose calculations are forever true."

"I see," Kelly replied, wondering if the Kasilians had regressed to the point that they had given up their intellectual capacity along with their technology.

"Do you number your people?" Dring asked. Apparently, he had already heard enough to adjust his pronunciation and grammar to venture a simple question.

Kelly was almost as impressed as the first time she saw him shape-shift from a toy-like dinosaur into a dragon.

"Yes, Ancient One," Kach replied, with a slight bow of his head. "Twice a year every district on Kasil holds a census festival, and the priests number all living things." Kach paused for a moment, and if Kelly didn't know better than to make assumptions about alien expressions, she would have said he looked a bit uncertain for the first time. "Of course, the counts of the beasts of the field, the creatures of the water and the things that fly in the heavens are based on small samples."

"Estimates," Kelly subvoced, but the voice box failed to translate the word. Perhaps it was taboo to introduce doubt in the counting? "Extrapolations," she tried again, a more accurate description in any case. This time, the word was translated.

The Kasilian clapped his hands and his eyes became noticeably brighter, such that Kelly was sure they would be visible in the dark. "Yes, extrapolations. I was cautioned that most people from other worlds use, uh, technology to do their thinking, so I was trying to speak with simple words."

"Good job, Kel," Joe murmured, nudging her in the side. "You've convinced the turnip farmer that you aren't a peat digger." Kelly glared at Joe, who immediately returned to his conversation with Mary. Across from Mary, Shaun was in a world of his own, studying the forest intently as if he expected to spot treasures hanging from tree branches.

"Is it permitted to tell the number of your people?" Dring followed up.

"It is a long number, like the trees of the forest," Kach replied. He held up four fingers of what Kelly now realized was a six-fingered hand, and raised his other hand in a closed fist. Then he rapidly raised and lowered a few fingers on both hands, showed another clenched fist, and repeated similar movements in quick succession, before letting his arms fall back to his sides.

"Forty-seven million, three hundred and twenty-six thousand, five hundred and thirty-two," Dring translated. "It's a Base-12 counting system, and the Kasilians have always avoided speaking large numbers out loud. At least that hasn't changed."

"On all of Kasil that's your total population?" Kelly asked Kach in shock. "There must have been a thousand times that many Kasilians when your people had colonies all over the galaxy!"

"The priests also tell us that," the Kasilian replied complacently. "But the visions of that time show that the people were unhappy, always at war with each other over possessions and desirable places to live. We even fought with other species where the Stryx allowed it. But when the great Prophet Nabay foretold the end for Kasil and shared it through vision speech, our people understood that all was vanity, that the only thing that matters is the Whole."

"Is that 'Whole' as in entirety, or 'Hole' as in empty space," Kelly asked, not wanting to misunderstand what could be the central concept of the Kasilian religion due to a homonym.

"Ah, so you are a philosopher!" Kach replied excitedly, his eyes shining like flashlights. "I apologize for thinking so poorly of you at first. I myself did not understand the duality of light and dark matter until I reached the eighth level of knowledge, and that didn't occur until I was a grandfather."

Kelly was beginning to suspect a glitch in the new translation tables since she understood all of the words Kach was saying, but his meaning didn't quite click. Maybe this was how it was with Becky and her inability to interpret the vision messages. She looked to Dring to see if he was equally puzzled, but the Maker was clearly satisfied with the progress of the discussion and enjoying himself immensely.

"I am happy to hear that your people retain their ancient love of cosmology," Dring remarked. "I spent many an interesting millennia studying the history of unseen space with your scholars of old. I hope you are not planning on giving away your telescopes with your other goods."

"Never!" Kach replied, as if shocked by the notion. "It's only the objects of envy that caused us so much sorrow in the days of old that we need to divest before achieving Unity. The jewels, precious metals, objects that were gathered from other species for the sake of hoarding wealth."

Snapping out of his reverie, Shaun was unable to contain his excitement. "You can rely on me to do everything I can to help relieve you of the burden," he declared, remembering to trigger his voice box this time. Mary looked a little embarrassed in the moment of silence that followed, but then Kach responded, and the deep emotional tone of his feeling was apparent even through the implant translation.

"Thank you," the Kasilian said.

Six

Aisha's slender body swayed gently as she scrubbed the pots after dinner. Although she still felt a lingering uneasiness when alone with Paul, she had prepared a large Indian meal the day after the fundraiser and kept doing so throughout the week. Paul came home to eat every night, after months of ordering take-out in his lab or eating out with Blythe when she was around. He claimed to be receiving subliminal messages about the meals, but Aisha assumed Paul was just following some sort of instructions from Kelly to keep her company.

There was an awkward exchange over who was to clean up after the first meal. Initially, Aisha gave in to Paul's insistence that he had been doing the dishes since he was taken in by Joe after being orphaned as a child. But she was so acutely uncomfortable watching a man doing kitchen work that she ended up hovering behind him and then rewashing everything when he finished. She gave Paul the excuse that she'd been doing the dishes since her wrists were strong enough to hold them, and that gave her seniority.

Paul usually headed back to his lab soon after the meal, but tonight he lingered in the kitchen and continued the dinner conversation with Aisha as he nursed a glass of beer. Strangely enough, he was barely aware of what Aisha was talking about, but somehow he could always catch just enough of the thread to say something that indicated he was paying attention. He felt hypnotized by her rhythmic movements as she worked through the surprisingly large collection of pots and saucepans she utilized to prepare a vegetarian meal. Paul had no reference to tell him that each night she was creating a holiday feast for two, using the freshest ingredients she could find on the Shuk deck first thing every morning. Some of the legumes required soaking all day before cooking.

"So until that awful competition, I always thought I would become a professional dancer," Aisha continued her narrative, scraping at a bit of seed husk stuck to a pan. She was accustomed to cooking certain dishes with ghee and she hadn't quite gotten used to the oil substitutes. "I'd always done well with the teacher bot, but there weren't any jobs in our village for sixteen-year-old girls who talked like they had swallowed a reference library. A couple of generations ago my parents could have married me off to some boy, but these days the young men all prefer signing labor contracts and leaving for space over settling down in the country with a teenage bride. And the truth is, I had a reputation for being a bit too aggressive for a girl," she added shyly.

"Aggressive? You?" Paul asked in disbelief, having registered the last few words. "You'll have to give me an example or I'll think you're just making it up."

Aisha looked over her shoulder at Paul and gave him a crafty smile. "Oh, I caused my parents enough problems, you know? They never would have agreed to my going off alone if I hadn't."

"I don't know," Paul replied jocularly, having entered fully in the conversation. "Let's hear some specifics."

"I asked too many questions about why we kept living the same way year after year," Aisha began. "Nobody liked it when I suggested changes to the traditional methods for doing things that I was sure would make life better. And when a factory farmer from the city began buying up hereditary fields from people who didn't have the legal right to sell them, I sent evidence to the local government and the media sites. After that, many of our neighbors stopped talking to me, and my parents barely let me out of the house for a whole year because they worried that it was unsafe."

Her voice went flat at this last statement, and her shoulders seemed to sag. Paul suddenly knew that her village life had not been the idyllic rural upbringing portrayed in the immersives. He rose to his feet and moved closer, wanting to donate his own strength to support her, but Beowulf raised his massive head and gave a warning growl.

"Not now, Killer," Paul told the dog crossly, and hesitantly extended a hand towards the girl's shoulder, thinking perhaps to give it an encouraging squeeze. The dog ventured a sharp bark and indicated the door with his nose, but Paul still didn't get the message. Then Blythe walked into the kitchen.

"Well, well, isn't this cozy," Donna's elder daughter commented in an artificially cheerful voice. Paul jerked back his hand and hid it in his pocket, while Aisha placed the last pot in the drying rack and turned to greet the new arrival.

"Please excuse my appearance," Aisha said, rapidly stripping off her pink rubber gloves. "I was just cleaning up after dinner, as you can see."

"Paul is way too old for an InstaSitter, and you're a little too tall to be one of Dorothy's playmates. Why don't you just tell me what you're doing here all alone with my boyfriend and then we'll all know how to act," Blythe replied in an angry rush, staring daggers at Paul the whole time.

"Boyfriend?" Aisha responded, looking at the pair in shock. "I didn't know, I mean, not that I have any right to ask such questions. I think perhaps I should leave?"

"If you're not going to answer, I'll get it out of this one," Blythe declared, poking Paul in the chest with a finger. "Would you care to explain how I find you making a move on a girl in the kitchen when your whole family is nowhere to be found?"

Aisha's sharp inhalation at Blythe's accusation brought Paul back to his senses, and he felt his own temper begin to rise. The scene was out of character for Blythe, but on returning to the station she had rushed to see Paul, even before going home to her sister and parents. Finding his lab empty, she had come ahead to Mac's Bones, still hoping to surprise him with her early return. It wasn't turning out to be the surprise she had planned for either of them.

"Your intelligence network must be breaking down if you didn't know the ambassador is off on a special mission for the Stryx," Paul answered sharply. "I thought pretty much every business-savvy ship owner in the galaxy was queued up at the tunnel entry, waiting for the go-ahead to plunder Kasil. And this is Aisha Kapoor, the new diplomatic intern for EarthCent. She's living in Laurel's old room."

Blythe recovered immediately after her first burst of emotion was spent, and she kicked herself for losing her poise for the first time in months. Two-plus years of running BlyChas Enterprises, a business that now operated on dozens of Stryx stations with millions of customers for the InstaSitter service, had developed her interpersonal skills to a scary degree. Paul once witnessed Blythe working her magic on a trio of Fillinduck parents whose child had unexpectedly molted out of season with nobody but a panicked young InstaSitter for company. Within months, it became fashionable among the Fillinduck upper classes to intentionally arrange for InstaSitters during molting.

"I apologize for losing my temper." Blythe turned back to Aisha with a friendly, if tightly controlled expression, and offered the girl a handshake. "I'm Blythe Doogal. You must know my mother Donna from the embassy. My only excuse is that I've been away from the station for an entire month, which is as long as I've gone without seeing Paul since we started dating three years ago."

"I understand how you feel," Aisha said. She shook Blythe's hand, reserving an accusatory look for Paul. "I've heard your mother talk so much about you, and your sister Chastity has helped me get settled into station life. We eat lunch together at least once a week. But nobody mentioned to me that you and Paul were engaged," she added, her breath suddenly short, as if she had tried reading one of Kelly's weekly reports out loud.

"Everybody around here is a joker," Blythe replied philosophically, taking a seat at the breakfast counter before Aisha's last word sank in. "Uh, and we're not engaged," she added quickly, finding herself rather startled by the misunderstanding. "I'll only be twenty on my next birthday, which is just twelve shopping days away in case somebody has forgotten. And I hope you'll come to the party, Aisha."

"You've been dating three years and you aren't even engaged?" Aisha asked, surprise overcoming her embarrassment and natural reticence at getting involved in discussions about other people's social norms. "Why, where I come from, you'd be married with two babies by now."

For Paul to be at a loss for words was nothing new, but for Blythe to open and close her mouth without speaking was virtually unheard of. Beowulf sat up to pay closer attention to the conversation, his massive head swinging from one human to the next, as if he was watching a tennis match.

"I'm sorry, I don't know anything about station society," Aisha apologized hastily for her unseemly question. "I've spent most of the past month just trying to figure out which of our alien friends can't stand the sight of each other, so I haven't had time to learn about the local human customs. Donna did mention that Kelly was thirty-five when she married Joe, and that it took an expensive Stryx dating service to make the match, so I suppose twenty is very young here."

"It's not a question of age," Blythe protested automatically. Running a galactic scale business in her teens had made her sensitive to any imputation of immaturity, one of her few weaknesses. "It's just that, well, we're only dating, you see?" she concluded awkwardly.

Aisha tried to see without success, and Beowulf looked equally puzzled. Unlike the humans, the dog found that scratching himself vigorously always put his mind at ease, after which he relaxed onto the floor in a sprawl.

"So, how was your trip," Paul broke the heavy silence in hopes of changing the subject. "Sign up any new franchisees?"

"Oh, it went fine," Blythe responded distractedly, even looking a bit puzzled at the mention of business. She studied Aisha closely, as if assessing a potential employee for InstaSitter, but then she shook the cobwebs from her brain and spoke with her usual decisiveness. "So you must have arrived on the station just after I left for my trip. How do you find working for EarthCent?"

"It's such an honor," Aisha replied, with the enthusiasm of a new recruit. "There's so much to learn, and the work is so important. I still can't believe that Kelly and your mother were the only full-time employees at the embassy. I'm talking with the Stryx as if they were just another family in the neighborhood. It's almost too much for me at times."

"I can imagine," Blythe responded sympathetically, having correctly categorized Aisha as country girl recruited through EarthCent's obscure no-application-required process. "I hope you'll tell me if there's anything I can do to help. We're all like a family here."

"Thank you so much," Aisha replied, feeling herself unwillingly won over by the force of Blythe's personality. Paul shifted uncomfortably on his feet, and Blythe rose from the breakfast counter stool.

"Well, I was going to take Paul out to dinner, but I guess I'm a little late for that tonight," Blythe said nonchalantly. "I should be getting home to see Chastity and my parents."

"I guess I should be getting back to the lab," Paul added quickly. "Thanks for dinner, Aisha. I'll be back late."

"It was so nice meeting you," Aisha told Blythe, pointedly ignoring Paul. "I'll be happy to attend your birthday celebration, and please tell me if I can bring anything."

"I'm glad I met you as well," Blythe responded, already planning to pump her mother and sister for details about the newcomer. "I'm sure we'll be seeing a lot of each other."

Seven

The delegation from Union Station waited nearly a week at Cathedral for the High Priest to return from a tour of regional monasteries. Kelly used the extra days on the ground to interview all of the local Kasilians willing to take time out from their labors, but none of them struck her as being repressed or dissatisfied with their form of government. To the contrary, Kasil appeared to be just the sort of agrarian paradise that many of the advanced species liked to fantasize about. Of course, those fantasies rarely included hauling well water by the bucket or shoveling dung by the cartload. Finally, the appointed day arrived, and they were told to expect a meeting with the High Priest after lunch.

"I'm going with Kevin and Becky to the candle-making place," Dorothy announced as soon as they finished their communal lunch. Kelly glanced at Becky to make sure the girl was actually part of the plan, and received a smile and a nod. The smaller children were fascinated by the dipping process, and would watch in rapt attention as the candles slowly grew fatter before their eyes. Cutting-edge astronomy and candle-making, Kelly thought to herself. What a combination.

"Have a good time," Kelly said to her daughter. "Just remember that wax is hot."

"I know that," Dorothy told her mother in exasperation. She pulled Kevin from the table just as the poor boy was reaching for another piece of the tasty purple fruit with the name that didn't translate into anything pronounceable.

"Is Metoo going with you?" Kelly asked, suddenly realizing she hadn't seen the little Stryx hovering around Dorothy lately.

"Don't think so," Dorothy answered with a shrug, which struck her mother as a bit heartless, given the years of devotion the robot had shown her daughter. But Kevin also lavished attention on the girl, and he had the advantage of being human and not quite as infuriatingly infallible as the young Stryx.

"Now that I think about it, I don't believe I've seen Metoo around at all the last couple days," Joe commented. "But I know Jeeves keeps tabs on him so I guess he's just looking around on his own."

"Maybe the poor little thing is feeling displaced by Kevin and is sulking," Mary suggested after the children left the room. Shaun coughed and looked embarrassed, causing his wife to grimace and address him sternly. "What did you do, Shaun Crick?"

"I didn't do anything," her husband protested. "I just asked the little fellow to keep his eyes open for opportunities to help the Kasilians."

"Help them with their wealth disposal problem," Mary said accusingly.

"Well that's what we're here for, darling, isn't it?" Shaun responded. He paused and looked around the table at his wife, the McAllisters, and Dring. "While the four of you run around playing at being cultural detectives, I have to be thinking about our future, don't I? I've kept my word not to accept any gifts until Kelly talks to this High Priest fellow after lunch, but there's no harm in scouting about a bit, especially when we'll be leaving tomorrow and the barbarians will come flooding in."

"So now you're the Prophet Nabay, that you can say what will happen tomorrow," Mary rebuked her husband. "I have full confidence our Kelly here will convince the High Priest to put everything on hold until she can report back to the Stryx. And the children like it here, it's a healthy place, so I'm in no hurry to be leaving."

"Welcome, honored guests," crooned an old Kasilian woman, who had quietly entered the room in the company of Jeeves. "I have been assured by Stryx Jeeves that you will understand my words through implanted translation devices, and can generate the Kasilian tongue through similar technology. I am High Priest Yeafah."

Kelly shot to her feet, followed instantly by Shaun and then the others, but the High Priest motioned with both of her hands that they should sit.

"Please, don't make such a fuss for an old woman," Yeafah continued. "I am sorry to have kept you waiting so long, though I can't imagine it mattered to you, Ancient One." She addressed this last missive to Dring with a glow in her eye.

"It has been many ages since I had the pleasure of speaking with a High Priest," Dring replied in the old tongue, giving the special ambassador a few extra seconds to pull her thoughts together. It didn't help.

"You're a woman," Kelly observed cleverly, and remained standing despite Yeafah's hint that they should seat themselves. "Oh, and I'm Kelly McAllister, the Stryx ambassador."

"I'm honored to meet you, Kelly McAllister. I didn't know that the Stryx were employing ambassadors from humanoid species," the High Priest replied politely. "I suspect that your translation devices misled you as to the nature of my office, but I assure you that I am both female and the High Priest."

"Of course," Kelly replied, taken off guard by the misalignment of her mental preparation with the actual facts. She had planned on saying something generous about the High Priest's appearance, an iron-clad rule from the first contact handbook, but the Kasilian was wearing a drab brown toga which exposed one ancient breast, and her fur was patchy in spots. Then Kelly's eyes caught a flash of crystal. "What a lovely necklace you're wearing. Is that your badge of office?"

"Please, take it," Yeafah replied, stripping off the necklace with an unexpected alacrity and stepping forward to press it into Kelly's hands. "There, there, now. Don't protest, you're doing me a great favor. Just put it on and let's see how it looks."

Kelly stammered an objection and tried to hand the necklace back, but the High Priest must have studied some sort of martial arts form involving wrist manipulations in her youth, because before Kelly knew it, the thin chain was slipped over her head and she was wearing the piece. Shaun took advantage of the commotion to slip from the room, but not before he caught his wife's eye and gave her a triumphant grin.

"Sit, all of you," The High Priest continued. "I conferred with the local priests when I arrived this morning, and they reported that you are brought here by multiple concerns for our well-being. Taking first things first, you are worried that our effort to divest ourselves of a meaningless accumulation of wealth will result in our world being overrun by the worst sorts of scoundrels."

"That's nowhere near as important as the survival of your species," Kelly objected immediately. "Yes, we're concerned that the gold rush may set off local fighting that could snowball into something bigger, and that your beautiful planet may be scarred in the process. But the real issue is the choice between life and death for you and your children."

"Please, slow down," Yeafah chided her. "By first things first, I meant to address your concerns in chronological order, not to rank them by importance. Of course our ultimate destination is more important than anything related to the disposal of material trinkets, but the final disassociation of the space through which Kasil travels is still years away."

"I've seen no indication of a police force on your world," Joe interjected, living up to his honorary role of military attaché. "Can you call on a militia if things get out of hand?"

"Ah, I see your point," Yeafah replied, turning to Kelly's husband. "No, we have lived in peace with one another since Prophet Nabay first calculated the path to transcendence. But the Sending to our Followers catalogued all of the objects that we wish to divest ourselves of, and we hoped our visitors could arrange the division of the goods beforehand. Is it your belief that there won't be enough for everyone who responds?"

"If you can ask that question seriously, you really have lost touch with how everybody else in the galaxy thinks," Kelly replied. "You are offering great wealth in return for simply showing up. Every valuable object that you give away will draw a hundred or a thousand new treasure seekers to your world. I have no doubt that the biggest wave will arrive after everything of value is gone, and they won't want to accept that they made the trip for nothing."

"Perhaps we have miscalculated the variables in this case," the High Priest admitted thoughtfully. "I see an ironic analogy between our position and that of our domestic animals, which after untold generations of breeding for farm life, are unsuited to spend even one night in the forest."

"There are already hundreds of vessels from dozens of species waiting at Stryx tunnel entrances for us to reopen your exit to the public," Jeeves reported. "And that's just the early birds, the ship owners who were willing to take a gamble on a historical legend. Ambassador McAllister is undoubtedly correct that when the first ships return home with your wealth, the numbers of incoming vessels will swell by orders of magnitude."

"That is alarming," Yeafah acknowledged calmly. "Yet, while I'm confident in the good will of the Stryx and the Ancient One, our collective memory holds no recollection of the species of your chosen ambassador." The High Priest nodded to Jeeves and Dring as she named them, and then addressed herself directly to Kelly. "Your outer appearance is close to that of a Vergallian, or perhaps a Drazen without the tentacle, but your aura is of a different order and there's a duality about you. May I ask who you are and how you became involved in our situation?"

"Our Earth was opened by the Stryx just two generations ago," Kelly explained. "One of our people on the station, this woman's daughter, received your Sending. I'm actually the EarthCent ambassador to Union Station, but I'm currently here for the Stryx because I'm detached."

"I see the Stryx made an excellent choice," the High Priest said approvingly. "Tricky situations are often best handled by individuals with no emotional involvement. Is your detachment achieved through rigorous professional training, or is it a characteristic of your species?"

"That didn't come out right," Kelly spluttered, "I'm really a very caring person, it's just my job I'm detached from. Oh, never mind what I mean. If we can get back to the problem at hand, this giveaway is going to turn your whole planet into a frontier town with battles in the streets. Is that really what you intended?"

"I believe her assessment, however unscientific, is a probabilistic near certainty," Dring offered in support.

"This is very unfortunate," Yeafah responded with a sigh. "While the continued presence of unwanted objects of desire can have no impact on the cosmological outcome of our path, we have long striven for consensus on ridding ourselves of such trappings. Now that we are finally all in agreement on divestiture, to remain burdened by unwanted wealth at the moment of transformation is unthinkable."

Kelly sat back, feeling that she had won the first point in a match. She tried to figure out the best way to bring up returning the High Priest's necklace, which featured a finger length crystal rod as a pendant. By an unspoken mutual decision, everyone waited patiently for Yeafah to come to a decision that was obviously painful for her. Suddenly, the High Priest's eyes shone with a light that forced the humans to look away, and even caused Dring to blink up the filters he engaged when welding, or gravity surfing too close to stars.

"If it wouldn't be too much of a burden for you, may I request transportation to Union Station so I can arrange for the disposal of our unwanted items there?" Yeafah asked hopefully. "Their bulk is less than you might think, since we spent all of our Stryx creds and bullion on restoring the surface of Kasil thousands of years ago."

"That would be no burden at all," Jeeves answered immediately, before Kelly even had a chance to open her mouth. "After you make the necessary arrangements, we will provide transport for your treasure, but I advise moving quickly. The expectation of our opening your tunnel exit has so far prevented ships from attempting to jump into your system, especially with the edge of the Darkness growing so near, but greed will eventually overcome fear."

"Wait a second," Kelly protested. "I thought we wanted the Kasilians to keep their stuff. And doesn't this just shift the riot to Union Station?"

"The decision to divest has already been taken," the High Priest reiterated firmly. "Would you rather we threw all of our museum collections into the sea?"

"Union Station can take care of itself," Jeeves added in support of Yeafah. "From what I know of humans, you should be more worried about complaints from your merchants that giving away shiploads of treasures will interfere with the functioning of the local markets."

"He's right about that," Joe interjected. "I've seen something similar happen after the sack of a royal treasury in war. When soldiers fill their pockets with gold and jewels, all of a sudden the price of a beer or a bed goes through the roof. It can wreak havoc on an economy, and the hard-working people who didn't load up on loot wake up to find they can't afford a loaf of bread."

"Since I have no experience in your galactic economy, I promise to be guided by your counsel when we reach the station. But I am still the spiritual leader here, although my term is drawing to a close. Before we leave, I shall officiate at the initiation ceremony of your comrade who has asked to join our priesthood, and I hope you will all attend," the High Priest concluded, and rising from her seat, exited the room.

"She can't mean Becky!" Kelly cried at Mary, who also appeared quite startled at Yeafah's pronouncement.

"I don't think so," Mary shook her head. "No, it can't be. Becky told me just this morning that the local priests were waiting for the High Priest to reverse the effects of the vision drug. Disassociation, they called it."

"Maybe some human took a crazy gamble and jumped into the system despite the odds," Joe speculated. "I knew plenty of guys who would have thought nothing of joining the priesthood for an inside track to the kind of treasure they're giving away."

"No ships have jumped into this system since we arrived, or for a very long time beforehand," Jeeves cut the speculation short. "And the members of the Kasilian priesthood must be highly proficient in both mathematics and astronomical observation at wavelengths that humans cannot detect without instrumentation."

"So it's not Shaun," Mary said, letting her breath out in relief.

"Are you leaving us, Dring?" Kelly asked the other half of her Victorian book club.

"No, I have my own path to follow," the Maker replied, sounding puzzled. "Process of elimination suggests just two possible candidates."

As if in answer to Dring's observation, Metoo floated in the door, draped in a brown toga that dragged on the floor.

Eight

"How am I going to explain to Stryx Farth that his son Metoo has joined the priesthood of a doomsday cult and remained behind on a suicide planet?" Kelly asked Libby, after she finally caught up with urgent correspondence when the delegation returned to Union Station.

"It will be a good experience for him," Libby told her. "I hope he decides to return to our school before his impressionable age passes, but it was already clear that he couldn't follow Dorothy around like a shadow forever. Besides, you don't have to explain anything. Farth knew about Metoo's decision before you did, and he heartily approves."

"But the Kasilians are just sitting there waiting for their world to come to an end," Kelly protested. "All they do is watch the Darkness approach, as if that makes any sense."

"I think it's very spiritual," Libby replied. "There are times I wish my Jeeves took a little more interest in the unknowable and a little less interest in practical jokes."

"Some of the artwork they're giving away is priceless," Kelly said to change the subject. "Bork already got in touch to tell me there are Drazen temple panels in the Kasilian catalog that were thought to be lost ages ago. Czeros absolutely flipped out over something that looked to me like an oversized straw hat. He said it could be the only example of a Frunge treaty weaving left in existence. The

Kasilians even have a complete image library of Gem from the days before cloning, not that the Gem are interested in them."

"The Kasilians were a very acquisitive species in their days of empire, and it seems they pruned their collection of artifacts to the most valuable pieces before retreating to their home world. I know we didn't have time to go over the history of Kasil before you left, but now that you've been there, would you believe their world was once a wasteland half-covered by metal-encased super-cities? You couldn't go outside without an environmental suit, and the flora and fauna were practically wiped out by millions of years of industrialization."

"It looked to me more like the world that time forgot," Kelly replied doubtfully. "Other than some astronomical observatories and gadgets, they appeared to be at the same level as Earth a couple thousand years ago."

"It shows what you can do, or undo, with enough money and time," Libby expanded on her thesis. "When the Kasilians began returning to their home world to wait for the end, they embraced the back-to-nature approach you see today. Most of the wealth they had accumulated over millions of years of spacefaring went into restoring Kasil. They were able to re-import strains of the original flora and fauna from their colony worlds, but the cost of remediation was stupendous. Even today you can find merchant families among the Dollnicks whose fortunes date back to trash-hauling contracts for the Kasilian clean-up."

"But why would they spend a fortune fixing up a planet just to have it destroyed?" Kelly asked in frustration. "No matter how I look at it, the whole thing doesn't make sense. Dring told me that the Kasilians were the galaxy's worst pessimists, and that the only things they believed in were wealth and astronomical observations. Then some prophet or mathematician comes along and proves that their home world is on a collision course with destruction some ten thousand years in the future. So why did they decide to give up all of their technology and go home to wait for species death? Why didn't they keep their wealth and their colonies and strip whatever was left of value from Kasil?"

"It was their unanimous choice," Libby replied. "Some races can reach a species consensus, as if they share a group mind. I can't tell you with any certainty why the Kasilians chose the path they did, though it's common for biologicals to wash the corpses of their dead before burial, so perhaps there's a parallel. I can only remind you that for all of their faults, the species you have encountered on Union Station are the stable ones. The Stryx have witnessed the rise and fall of uncounted sentient species, some who never leave their planet of birth and others who spread across the galaxy and beyond. At a certain point in their development, many intelligent species find that their evolution has left them spiritually, or you might say, psychologically unsuited to their place in the universe. Some find peace by going home, others by stepping back from technology or breaking all ties with their home world and starting anew. Unfortunately, a large proportion of biologicals simply reach a peak and then go into decline, often to the point of extinction."

"It looks to me like the Kasilians have doubled-down on extinction," Kelly said sourly. "Even if Kasil isn't eaten by their precious Darkness, the entire population of the planet wouldn't fill half of Union Station."

"Knock, knock?" Aisha called from the door, peering around the corner, as was her habit.

"Come in, come in," Kelly replied in relief. A nice chat with the naïve intern would be a welcome break from discussing the extinction of a species. "How was the fundraiser? Did Paul treat you well?"

Aisha looked a bit flustered for a moment, which in combination with her cheap coveralls, made her look like a lost schoolgirl who was late for her part-time service job. Kelly resolved on the spot to send her shopping with Donna, who had years of experience getting her own fashion-indifferent daughters to dress like adults.

"The fundraiser was very strange," Aisha finally replied. "I spoke a little with the Drazen and Frunge ambassadors, who were very friendly, but they also seemed to be making fun of us. They put on some sort of skit they called an EarthCent Ambassador game, and it drew quite an audience. Then the Vergallian ambassador tried to, uh, to befriend Paul, and I'm afraid I was a little rude to her."

"I know what kind of friends the Vergallian women try to make of human men. Pets is a better description," Kelly remarked scornfully. To avoid explaining the Drazen and Frunge theatrical production, she resorted to a little teasing. "And did Paul behave himself as a gentleman?"

"Why didn't you tell me he is dating Blythe?" Aisha asked suddenly, sticking out her bottom lip in the closest thing to a confrontational expression Kelly had ever seen on her intern. "It was very embarrassing to have her walk into the kitchen when I was alone with Paul after dinner. It made me feel like a pracanda mahila, a wanton woman."

"Nobody mentioned that Paul and Blythe are a couple?" Kelly asked in surprise, not noticing Aisha's wince at the term. "I suppose we're all so used to them dating that we take it for granted that everybody knows, and she was probably away on business from the time you arrived on the station. But to tell you a secret," Kelly lowered her voice conspiratorially, "I'm not so sure that she's good for Paul. He's always let her boss him around a little too much."

"Really?" Aisha perked up immediately. "I was surprised that they aren't even engaged after dating for three years. It seems like an awfully long time to wait for people who love each other."

"Joe and I got married on our first date," Kelly replied instantly, as it wasn't something she often had the chance to boast about. "Of course, I was a bit tipsy. But the fundraiser and one dinner with Paul didn't take up your whole week. What else did I miss?"

"Well," Aisha replied, thinking to herself that it wasn't just one dinner, "I took your weekly meeting with the Earth merchants from the Shuk and the guilds this morning. They had all heard about the Kasilian offer by then, and word was already out that the High Priest was accompanying you back to the station to dispose of Kasil's wealth here."

"Libby?" Kelly inquired, turning her eyes upward. "How is it that everybody knew we were coming back with Yeafah when the Kasilian's only communications technology relies on visions?"

"We had to tell all of the ship captains waiting at the tunnel entrance something or they would have clogged up the shipping lanes forever," Libby replied. "Most of them chose to come directly to the station, and I have no doubt that Joe has a few new campers."

"What did the merchants who attended the meeting have to say?" Kelly asked, looking back to Aisha.

"They all had different opinions about how the Kasilians dumping their wealth on the station would affect business, but as I understood it, the main problem is uncertainty," Aisha reported. "Because it's something they've never experienced, they don't know how to prepare for it. They feel like they have no control over the situation. I'm afraid many of them blame you and EarthCent for bringing the problem here rather than keeping it on Kasil."

"Our merchants are a tough bunch," Kelly said sympathetically. "I hope they weren't too hard on you."

"It was a little scary at first," Aisha admitted. "But then I told them the story about how my family's business changed after the elevators opened, and super-cheap textiles from the robotic orbital factories around the galaxy flooded the market. My mother convinced my father to let the old business go and to refocus on hand-made clothing for weddings and the luxury market. It was hard for the first few years, but now they are starting to do well for the first time in their lives. One woman who owns a clothing boutique on the retail deck even asked me for their contact information."

"If the merchants like you that much, maybe you should take over the weekly meetings," Kelly offered with a smile.

"What will the High Priest do now?" Aisha asked, emboldened by the praise and a week of working on her own.

The ambassador was surprised and pleased that Aisha had finally asked her a question without first asking for permission. Kelly had been considering a clandestine course of aggressiveness training for her overly polite intern, such as a trumped up undercover assignment working with the Hadads in the Shuk or with Donna's girls at InstaSitter. The girl was obviously intelligent and always looked like she had something to say, but she rarely opened her mouth unless Kelly asked her a question. Maybe she was starting to come around on her own.

"I wish I could tell you," Kelly replied. "The whole trip was something of a disaster from my point of view. Did you know that Metoo joined the Kasilian priesthood and stayed behind? I don't think it's really hit Dorothy yet, but don't be surprised if you see her moping around the house. I only hope that the Cricks stay around a while longer, because without Kevin, the poor girl will have lost all of her admirers."

"The High Priest didn't say anything about his intentions?" Aisha followed up, displaying the ability to remain focused on the point.

"She, not he," Kelly responded. "Her name is Yeafah. I'm not sure it's even a religion, exactly, despite the priesthood. It's just the closest translation to English. Dring explained that some species have concepts for which there simply isn't an equivalent in human experience, so the translation implants just pick something that's related."

"So did Yeafah say anything about her intentions?" Aisha persisted stubbornly.

"She mainly talked about fish and birds," Kelly admitted. "The Kasilians see the restoration of their planet's natural cycles that were lost in their hyper-industrial age as their great achievement. But the way she tells the stories, they all end in death. The fish return home to their streams and die. The birds fly around the world with the seasons and die. The great herds circle the plains and die. The forest creatures—you get the picture."

"But that's Samsara, the circle of life," Aisha protested. "With death comes rebirth, it's never-ending."

"Not in the Kasilian version," Kelly retorted grimly. "Dring explained that their whole system, whether you call it religion or government, was founded on the discovery that their star system is doomed. Astronomical observations have been the uniting passion of Kasilians from time immemorial, perhaps because Kasil has no moon and their location in the galaxy makes their night sky brilliant. You know that on Earth there are amateur astronomers who hunt for comets?"

"Yes," Aisha replied briefly, wondering if there was a point to her superior's discursion.

"On Kasil, all adults spend several hours a night studying the heavens, and they took the tradition with them when they began colonizing other worlds. But it turns out that stargazing was their only likeable characteristic. They were rapacious in business, fought wars amongst themselves to acquire property and slaves, and only tolerated other species when they could see an economic advantage. They were major players on the galactic stage for a few million years, but then they went into sharp decline, a sort of collective mental break-down, as Dring described it."

"But what does this have to do with their world being doomed?" Aisha demanded with uncharacteristic impatience.

"I'm getting there," Kelly replied, amused that Aisha could have changed so much in just a week. "A Kasilian scientist who became known as Prophet Nabay spotted a sort of a gravitational distortion moving through space, on a course that would eventually intercept their star system. Of course, space is so vast that even large objects like black holes and stars can pass through occupied systems, with the main danger being from gravitational effects. But Nabay showed that this distortion, which the Kasilians call the Darkness, was something else altogether. It's more than large enough to swallow up entire star systems, and where it traveled, it left empty space in its wake."

"What do the Stryx say about it?" Aisha asked.

"I told Joe to ask Jeeves and then to explain it to me," Kelly answered. "He said that they call it Darkness because it's made of stuff that you can't see, but the Kasilians can detect its path indirectly because it bends the light from other stars. Joe said that human science hasn't yet developed the models to describe Darkness, anymore than we can understand how the tunnels or jump engines work. He also said that we've known for almost a century that the universe mainly consists of matter and energy we can't see, and that this is some of it."

"Can the Stryx fix it?" Aisha couldn't help asking.

"They aren't omnipotent," Kelly replied. "Saving the Kasilians isn't a problem if the Kasilians will only go along with it. There are so few of them at this point that they would all fit on a Stryx station like this one, with room for twice as many more. Jeeves said that given enough time, the Stryx could have used gravitational towing to move Kasil to a new star system. But it's extremely complicated to do with a world that's occupied, because you have to provide heat and light on the trip, essentially an artificial sun. The Stryx could have done it if they started when Nabay first discovered the Darkness, but there isn't anywhere near enough time remaining."

"So their religion or government, which sees death as the end of the natural cycle, won't allow the Stryx to help?" Aisha persisted doggedly. "And the people all do what the High Priest tells them? It sounds like she would be a very depressing travel companion."

"Surprisingly not," Kelly said with a laugh. "In fact, aside from the whole dying business, she's actually very upbeat. In any case, you'll be meeting her soon because she's staying with Dring while she's on the station."

"Knock, knock," Donna said as she walked into the office. She only did it when Aisha was present, and Kelly wasn't sure whether the embassy office manager was trying to make their intern comfortable, or poking gentle fun at her. "How was your vacation?"

"It wasn't a vacation," Kelly objected immediately. "I worked the whole time I was there. But I couldn't talk the High Priest out of giving away all of their wealth. Apparently, they reached a perfect consensus through their vision-speak that it's the right thing to do."

"I see," Donna commented dryly. "Nice necklace."

Nine

After two days of consultations and outright arguments, Kelly gave in and agreed to sponsor the Kasilian High Priest's giveaway conference. Dring did most of the pushing, but the Stryx also dropped some heavy hints about how establishing a good relationship with Yeafah might save tens of millions of lives later down the road. Kelly also felt a certain guilty obligation to Shaun Crick, who had come away from Kasil with nothing after the High Priest changed her mind. So far, Kelly's necklace was the only bit of treasure the Kasilians had actually given away, and failing to persuade Yeafah to accept its return, Kelly had stopped wearing it.

Donna arranged the rental of the Galaxy room at the Empire Convention Center for the event. The Galaxy room incorporated two half-amphitheatres, without the central partition that allowed them to be rented for separate events. It featured Coliseum-style seating, though in place of stone, the steps were formed from a plastic variant that had a little give to it. The full amphitheatre could have held around five thousand humans, but most alien species needed a little more room. With Libby's help, Donna held a lottery for the tickets to attend in person, and arranged with Gryph to broadcast the event on the Union Station feed. The attendees all arrived early to get the best seats, making Kelly wonder if they imagined that the High Priest would stand on the stage with a box of jewels and scatter them into the crowd.

While waiting for Dring to show up with Yeafah, Kelly silently went over the speech she had prepared for the occasion. "First, I'd like to welcome to Union Station those of you who are guests here. We are gathered today because the High Priest of Kasil, the official and sole legal representative of the Kasilian people, has come to dispose of certain items that her people have come to see as burdens. All of you have seen the catalog, so you know that in addition to artworks and other valuables, the list includes historical artifacts from Kasilian museums that are of great value to some of the species present. I hope we can all act with restraint and good-will to see that these cultural treasures are restored to the descendents of their creators, rather than disappearing into private collections."

"There's been a change in plan," Libby spoke over her implant.

"WHAT?" Kelly subvoced, as her head snapped up she began searching for the nearest exit. "Is this why you all wanted me to sponsor the event? You dragged me into a Coliseum and now you're going to throw me to the wild beasts?"

"It's a good change," Libby reassured her. "I know you were deeply concerned about the complaints from human merchants, and all of the business leaders of the species represented on the station felt the same way. It took Dring and Jeeves up to the last moment to bring Yeafah around to seeing things from our perspective, but she finally accepted a compromise."

"Tell me she's agreed to give the stuff away somewhere else," Kelly said hopefully.

"Noooo," Libby drew out the vowel, giving the EarthCent ambassador time to adjust. "It's a more fundamental change than that. Yeafah has agreed that it would be irresponsible on her part to simply give away all of their wealth to strangers on a first-come, first-serve basis. Your idea of sending Shaina to talk to Yeafah about disruptions to local trade and then getting Blythe to brief her on the station network economy must have done the trick. Jeeves tells me she was very taken by both young women."

"Well, that's great, Libby," Kelly replied cautiously. "So why do I get the impression that you're about to drop a giant shoe on my head?"

"The important thing from Kasilian perspective is that they rid themselves of the burden," Libby continued. "But she also didn't want to disappoint the adventurers who came from all over the galaxy after hearing about the Sending, something the High Priest regards as an act of faith. So you're going to hold an auction instead."

"An auction? I suppose that solves the immediate problem, though it will leave her with a mountain of Stryx creds to get rid of," Kelly replied. "But wait a minute. Did you say that I'm going to hold the auction? As in, ME?"

"In order to get her to go along with the idea, Yeafah insisted that somebody take legal possession of their goods immediately, and receive the money from the auction without it returning into Kasilian hands. She feels she would be failing to carry out the wishes of the Kasilian consensus otherwise," Libby explained.

"Okaaay," Kelly drawled in return, while she began arranging arguments to reject the assignment. "Do I need to ask who is about to become one of the richest and most loathed individuals in the galaxy?"

"We didn't have a choice," Libby replied apologetically. "Kasilian law only recognizes a property transfer if something of value is given and accepted as a token of the larger transaction. If it hadn't been for the necklace Yeafah gave you, it would have taken another trip back to Kasil just to complete the contract."

"But I never agreed to it!" Kelly objected.

"Please, Kelly," Libby implored, with real emotion apparent in her synthesized voice. "Gryph was already prepared to impose a similar solution in the name of protecting the peace. It's why Jeeves was so anxious to get the High Priest to Union Station where we could control the situation. I'm sorry we couldn't tell you ahead of time, but we wanted to avoid interfering directly, and in the end, you provided both the persuasion and the solution without Gryph having to act."

"But what am I supposed to tell all of these aliens who showed up for freebies?" Kelly asked, temporarily resigning herself to the Stryx plan.

"That's the good news," Libby told her. "We informed all of the attendees that it would be an auction before they came. We just couldn't tell you, or you would have given up on convincing Yeafah to change her mind and never sent the girls to talk to her. Speaking of which, Shaina is coming to help you with the auction. She's just leaving Dring's ship in Mac's Bones now, so you can either start yourself or tell everyone to be patient for a couple more minutes. I just wanted to give you the maximum amount of notice."

"I may as well just start," Kelly grumbled. "I can't imagine we'll get through the whole catalog today, but please send Aisha to help as well, and whoever else you can trick into coming."

"Thank you, Kelly," Libby replied enthusiastically. "I'll project the holo catalog images above the stage and keep track of the buyers for you. The catalog description for each item will come up on your heads-up display. You're the best."

Kelly walked in a small circle around the podium, letting the noise wash over her and scanning the thousands of alien faces for a friend or acquaintance. She didn't recognize a soul. A loud chime sounded and a holographic representation of something that looked like a hairpin for a giant with a pearl the size of a cantaloupe popped into existence over her head. The crowd fell silent. Kelly had no idea whether it was in fact a hairpin or a very expensive harpoon, because there was nothing in the hologram to indicate the scale.

Kelly was about to start reading the description of the first object from her heads-up display, when it occurred to her that most of the little speech she'd memorized would work for an auction as well as a free-for-all. She mentally edited out the line about the High Priest, routed her subvoc pick-up into the room's public announcement system, and delivered the remainder of the speech with as much enthusiasm as she could muster. Failing to receive even a polite round of applause in response, she gave-up on delaying tactics and began to read from the ghostly cue cards.

"The first item in our auction is a jeweled Horten worm prod from the Phyrgixx Brxxid period," she stumbled through unpronounceable words. Fortunately, all of the attendees could read the descriptions on their own heads-up displays, and only the Hortens would really know how badly she was massacring their language. "Will somebody offer, uh, two hundred Stryx creds?" she hazarded a guess.

"Done," cried nearly a hundred quick-thinking aliens at once, nearly rupturing her eardrums so she didn't register the ensuing round of laughter. Well, Kelly thought to herself, Libby said she would track the buyers, so I can just move on.

"The next item," she began, and then realized that the same hologram was still in place over the stage, and that the description projected on her heads-up display hadn't changed.

"You have to take bids," shouted a giant Dollnick seated on the fake stone step in front of her.

"What?" Kelly asked reflexively. "Oh right, an auction. I remember now. Um, does somebody else want to bid?"

"You have to say, 'I have two hundred. Do I hear three hundred?' and then point at the next bidder," a human she didn't recognize called out from the side of the Dollnick.

"Oh, I get it," Kelly replied. "I'll just warn you that I've never really been to an auction before." There was a collective groan from the crowd at this revelation. "Alright then. I have two hundred. Do I hear three hundred?"

"Done," shouted a smaller group of comedians, drawing another wave of laughter. But then Kelly heard a voice behind her call, "Three hundred," and she spun around.

"Great, three hundred!" she exclaimed. "Who said that?"

A sea of aliens raised a hand, waved a tentacle or twitched an ear, depending on their cultural approach to auctions.

"Come on," Kelly pleaded. "You have to cooperate with me here. Don't you want this to work?"

"It's the Ambassador Game," shouted somebody who must have been a local diplomat, and the whole hall erupted in hysterics. Fortunately, by the time the laughter died down and the attendees were ready for serious business, Shaina showed up with her sister Brinda. The two petite women in their mid-twenties took over immediately.

"What's the bid," Shaina asked Kelly, glancing at the hologram. Before Kelly could answer, the young woman put her hands on her hips and bellowed at the crowd, "Hey, keep your pants on out there or you're going to find out how these worm prods worked the hard way!"

"Three hundred," Kelly replied mournfully in the ensuing silence. "But I don't know who offered it. Libby said she would keep track of the buyers."

"Libby meant the winners, and we need more spotters," Shaina told the EarthCent ambassador decisively. "A few dozen of them would be good. In the meantime, you take this section, between that pink Grenouthian and the Vergallian bombshell. Brinda, you have from the bombshell to the sad-looking Thark fellow. Kelly, when somebody in your section shouts a bid or makes a gesture, you point at them and repeat the price so we all know. Tell Libby to send more spotters, and ask her who's taking the offsite bids."

"I'll handle them," Jeeves replied as he arrived on the central stage. "Gryph is about to push the feed out on Stryxnet, so anybody with access to a ship controller or a Stryx cred register can submit real-time bids. Most of the bidders in the room have already been recruited to act as agents of the institutional buyers for their respective species, so the Thark recorders had a busy afternoon. And Kelly, the High Priest wanted you to know that we announced a free tunnel transit plus a ten thousand cred rebate on the first purchase for the early arrivals, so they should all be in a good mood."

"I make the worm prod two hundred thousand, minimum," Brinda commented, while studying the aliens in her section.

"Brinda concentrated in Art and Artifacts at the Open University," Shaina told Kelly. "She glanced through the catalog and the values are all over the place, from under ten thousand creds on some jewelry, to over a billion for some of the one-of-a-kind museum pieces. We're going to have to skip over the less expensive items and group them into lots for later, or the auction will go on for months."

"Months?" Kelly asked, dumbfounded. "How many items are there?"

"You don't want to know," Shaina replied with a happy grin. "Just be glad that the Kasilians aren't including their personal ornamentation in the deal or it would be a thousand times as much. The catalog is all high-end stuff, there's just an awful lot of it."

"Alright ladies, we're live across the galaxy," Jeeves informed them, sounding about as excited as Kelly had ever heard him.

"Two hundred thousand!" Shaina sang out suddenly, her unamplified alto penetrating to the highest benches of the amphitheatre. "Two hundred thousand, starting two, give me two, two?" she paused and pointed at a Dollnick in her section. "Bid two. Now three hundred. Will you give me three? Two hundred, bid two, go three? Now two-fifty. Give me two-fifty?"

"Two-fifty," shouted Brinda, pointing at a Horten in her section whose face was glowing orange with excitement.

"Two-fifty, now three. Will you go three? Two-fifty, give me three? Now two-seventy-five. Give me two-seventy-five," Shaina chanted, going faster and faster as she warmed to the task.

"Three!" Kelly called, pointing at a Frunge in the second row of her section.

"Three hundred thousand," Shaina continued. "I have three, now three-twenty-five. Three-twenty-five."

"I was just scratching my head!" protested the Frunge loudly, causing Kelly to cringe in embarrassment.

"Bid two-seventy-five," Shaina continued without missing a beat. "Now three, will you give me three? Now three, higgley dee, will you give me three?"

"Three," Jeeves thundered, clearly getting into the auction spirit.

"Three hundred thousand," Shaina revisited the bid. "Now three-twenty-five. Will you give me twenty-five? Twenty-five? Now twenty? Give me twenty? Now ten? I have ten," she pointed at a Horten in her own section. "Three hundred and ten, now fifteen? Give me fifteen? Going once. Going twice. Sold, to the handsome Horten for three hundred and ten thousand Stryx cred. Brinda?"

"Our next lot is a Kraaken gold and depleted uranium icon with natural Thrump tusk inlay. Due to environmental regulations, this item may not be imported into the Kraaken confederacy," Brinda read from the catalog description, double-checking that the hologram displayed over the heads agreed with the entry. "Starting five hundred thousand, five hundred. Gimme five, go five, gimme five. Four hundred. Now four hundred. Go four hundred."

"Four hundred?" Kelly pointed at an alien in an environmental suit who she believed was a native of Theodric. The helmeted head nodded in confirmation.

"I have four, four hundred thousand, go five," Brinda started back in, her words running together so fluently that Kelly wondered how the translation implants of the aliens kept up. "Gimme five, now five, bid four, gimme five."

"Five," Jeeves trumpeted, and all of a sudden the current bid was floating under the giant hologram of the Kraaken icon, which was rotating slowly to give everybody in the amphitheatre a view.

"Bid five, gimme six, now six," Brinda continued at a break-neck pace. Kelly scanned her section for movement, starting to raise her arm to point more than once, only to decide the potential bidder was just shifting in place.

"This is hard," Kelly subvoced at Libby. "We really need those spotters."

"On the way," Libby replied. "And you have six, Kraaken in the middle of your section wearing the purple poncho. He's yelling 'six' but they have weak voices."

"Six," Kelly shouted immediately, pointing at the purple poncho.

"Have six, six hundred thousand. Now seven, will you give me seven? Bid six, will you go seven? Now six-fifty, will you go six-fifty? Bid six, now six-twenty-five, can I get twenty-five? Now twenty-five. No? Bid six, I'm letting it go. Once, twice, sold!"

"Cavalry's here," Libby spoke over Kelly's implant, as the Hadad girls put their heads together and fast-forwarded through a couple dozen of the lower value items in the catalog. Led by Chastity, nearly a hundred InstaSitters, mainly teenage girls from the various species, began spreading out through the Galaxy room. They spaced themselves on the stairs that radiated from the central stage up the tiered bench seating, so that each InstaSitter had at most fifty bidders to watch.

"Do you want to try again?" Shaina asked Kelly. "This is a good one, a Sun Temple panel from Hoong Prime. Brinda says the textbooks claim the originals were all lost or destroyed in a war millions of years ago. Those Kasilians sure knew how to hoard. We're going to start it at a hundred million, but it could go for billions if the Hoong foundations get involved."

"A hundred million!" Kelly blanched. If Shaina had been offering her a microphone she would have pushed it away. "No, you and Brinda are doing great. I'll just work on my bid reporting. Maybe Chastity would like to try later."

Shaina nodded and then cranked her voice back up to operatic volume. "Moving to item sixty in the catalog. All items we skip over will be assembled in lots for a post-auction session. Early responders to the Sending who don't use their credit on a more expensive item will have a chance to bid separately on items from lots that don't make the reserve bid."

A hologram of a group of panels depicting a primitive battle scene, featuring aliens Kelly didn't recognize but which she assumed were Hoongian gods and mythical creatures, appeared floating over the stage. The panels were carved in some type of white stone that was fine-grained like marble and heavily gilded with precious metals set with gemstones. The work was clearly a cultural treasure, and unless the Hoongians were indifferent to their history, Kelly was sure they would be the buyers at any price.

"Item sixty is a complete set of Sun Temple panels from Hoong Prime," Shaina read the description, and paused for a moment out of respect for the artistic labor that had clearly gone into their making. Then she plunged into her chant, starting at a hundred million, as if she auctioned off unique artifacts worth more than a fleet of spaceships every day.

"Start at one hundred million, do I have—now two hundred," she interrupted herself, taking a bid from the front of her own section. "Now two hundred, I have two, now five hundred, now a thousand," Shaina ramped up without blinking as she picked up bids from aliens without having to wait for the spotters. "A thousand million, now one billion Stryx cred," she reset the chant. "Now one, give me one."

Kelly had once asked Jeeves how many Stryx cred billionaires there were in the galaxy, and the robot had told her that most industrial worlds had a dozen or so. The home worlds of the more advanced species usually boasted a few trillionaires, though their assets weren't liquid. So the amount of money Shaina was asking for the panels was inversely related to the population that could dream of bidding. Maybe one in a billion sentient beings had that kind of money or credit at their disposal. And it was all to be deposited to her name?

"One billion!" Jeeves reported, and this time he threw in a bell-ringing noise.

"Bid one, now two, can I have two?" Shaina continued, swiveling her head about to watch the spotters in the crowd.

"Two billion!" Jeeves reported, causing the amount under the hologram to flash, and ringing the virtual bell twice.

For the next six hours, Kelly performed mechanically, calling bids from the rows right in front of her and

93

occasionally repeating bids from spotters in her section who didn't have loud voices, but it was clear that she wasn't cut out for the auction business. Chastity declined a turn at bid calling, saying that it made no sense for an amateur to interrupt professionals at their jobs. When the Hadad girls called it quits at midnight, they had worked through a fifth of the catalog, though they were skipping past nine out of ten items to be lumped into lots for later.

"Why aren't you exhausted?" Kelly asked Brinda in wonder, noticing that the young woman simply looked energized.

"This is the chance of a lifetime, a thousand lifetimes," she replied with shining eyes, and Kelly suspected she might have even detected a tear. "I can't thank you enough for giving me this opportunity. I may never be able to own or even touch artifacts like these, but you've made me part of their history."

"It's been a blast," Shaina added. "I told my dad he's on his own for the next week or so, though the truth is, it's going to be hard going back to the Shuk and selling egg-slicers for centees after auctioning off a trillion creds of fine art and artifacts to the wealthiest institutions and collectors in the galaxy. Is that your total, Brin?"

"I lost track around five hundred billion," Brinda admitted. "I thought those big numbers only came up in physics. So what are you going to do with it all, Kelly? Buy a couple worlds?"

"Do with it?" Kelly repeated. At some point in the long evening she had forgotten that she was the legal beneficiary of the auction. Her last raise as EarthCent ambassador had brought her annual salary up to six thousand Stryx cred, and she and Joe had around eight thousand in hard-earned savings between them. Kelly desperately searched the stage for some dark corner before running out of time and throwing up directly under the hologram of the last item sold, a ten-ton golden bunny that had driven the Grenouthians into a bidding frenzy.

"I'll call a maintenance bot," Jeeves offered kindly. "You can thank me for suggesting that Yeafah make you the beneficiary when you're feeling better."

Ten

Shaun returned to Mac's Bones from the last day of the odd lots after-auction in a much better mood than he'd been in since they initially set out for Kasil three weeks earlier. He'd come away from the planet empty-handed, thanks to Dring, Jeeves and Kelly talking the High Priest into returning to Union Station before making a decision, but he'd received a ten-thousand cred voucher towards the auction for being an early bird. By waiting for the final lots, he'd managed to convert his bidding credit into gold at very near the market price. While ten thousand Stryx creds wasn't the treasure he'd dreamed of, it was the largest windfall the Crick family had ever seen.

The McAllisters were throwing a post-auction party for all of the staff, which by this point included over three hundred InstaSitters who had been hired as spotters for the eight sessions it took to work through the catalog. Kelly hadn't returned to the center stage after the first night, but the Hadad sisters and Jeeves were the ones who really ran the auction in any case, and the three of them had the time of their lives. Jeeves had surprised everybody by developing his own auction chant, complete with nonsense words for maintaining the rhythm, and a concluding cry of, "Sold!" that made the phony stone benches in the amphitheatre vibrate.

Kelly and Aisha helped the crew hired from Laurel's old culinary college set up for the picnic, while Beowulf got in a final nap before the action began. Chastity and Tinka also came early to help, and they greeted the InstaSitters as they arrived, basically hijacking the party as a BlyChas event. With Blythe traveling so often, Tinka had become Chastity's right hand, and in addition to the kind of salary that Kelly could only dream of, the girls had given the Drazen a small equity stake in the business.

Shortly after the tables filled up with InstaSitters and the grills started going full force, Shaina and Brinda arrived with Jeeves in tow. The young spotters broke into a rousing cheer. Joe approached the Hadads as soon as they were seated and presented each of them with a pint of his latest ale.

"Worst crowd we've ever had for beer drinkers," he complained to the auctioneers, who along with Chastity, Tinka, Shaun, Mary, Kelly and Aisha, made up a grown-ups table. "Kelly suggested I start brewing a small beer for kids, which sounded great until I found out it was Medieval euphemism for low-alcohol. What does InstaSitter have against hiring adults?"

"Kids work cheaper and have much more flexible schedules on the stations," Tinka explained. "Besides, if we hired adults as sitters, they'd probably need to call us to look after their children or parents while they worked, so they may as well stay home and save everybody the overhead."

"I love your approach to business," Shaina complimented the InstaSitter management team. "It's no wonder you guys have been so successful. And the kids worked out great as spotters. It really helps to have a whole variety of species who can learn the difference between a twitchy whisker and a bid."

"Well, you did such a great job you must be ready to retire after the last week," Chastity returned the compliment. "What's the auctioneering commission on a sale like that? I hadn't even thought of it, but you guys must be the richest people on the station now. After Kelly, I mean."

Kelly opened her mouth to protest, but quickly closed it again as she felt a surge of nausea. She took a sip from Joe's half-finished beer, hoping it would calm her stomach so she could eat something, but she hadn't been this queasy since she was pregnant with Dorothy. Waking up a trillionaire because the High Priest of Kasil had used martial arts to force a necklace on her was enough to give anybody an upset stomach. Why did the universe have to be so weird?

"We weren't working on commission," Brinda replied cheerfully. "Shaina didn't think it would be right, since we really aren't professionals and my appraisals were just off-the-cuff guesses. The Kasilian catalog really did most of the work for us. Besides, we're too young to retire, though I'm not sure I can go back to work in the Shuk selling kitchen gadgets now."

"I would have paid Kelly for the opportunity to run that auction," Shaina confessed. "Anyway, we took the job from Libby in return for Gryph waiving the Kitchen Kitsch rent for the next two years. Still, I feel a little like an athlete who isn't even thirty yet and knows that her best days are behind her."

"That's not so," Aisha protested. "I mean, you did a beautiful job and aliens all over the galaxy recognize you for it, but none of us had even dreamed of this auction two weeks ago. Your business in the Shuk is something you've worked at building all of your lives."

"She has a good point," Shaun chipped in unexpectedly after polishing off his burger. "I've been a bit crazy since our Becky told us about the Kasilian intentions, but truth be told, we just got lucky. It'll be nice to buy some things for the kids, but I'm glad I'm not in Kelly's shoes."

"Shush up now," Mary told her husband with a glance at their hostess. But the comment had gone unnoticed by Kelly, who was occupied by a chiming in her ear and the message "Collect call from mom," floating across her vision.

"Accept charges," she subvoced in a grumble. "Hi, Mom. I thought you were all done with this collect call nonsense."

"What? Has my daughter turned into a cheapskate in her middle age?" Her mom's voice sounded incredulous. "You could buy and sell me a million times over. You could probably buy the tunneling communications network from the Stryx and then I could call for free!"

"Don't exaggerate, Mom. It's just a few trillion creds," Kelly replied, instantly realizing how lame that sounded.

"Well, I'm glad you haven't lost your sense of perspective yet," her mother replied in an ironic singsong. "You're one of the richest people in the galaxy now, though if it had been me, I would have held onto some of that Vergallian jewelry you sold in the small lots. Such beautiful work."

"It's not my money," Kelly retorted, then backtracked. "I mean, it's legally mine, but I'm just doing the Stryx a favor by accepting it. I'm sure they'll tell me what to do with it soon."

"Did they tell you not to spend it?" her mother inquired.

"That's not the point," Kelly protested desperately. "Libby knows me better than I know myself. She set me up with Joe, remember? They're just playing one of their noninterference games, but I'm sure in a few days, I'll get a hint that there's a nebula in need of renovations or something."

"A nebula in need of—Kelly, you know even less about space than you do about business," her mother chided her. "I just wanted to check in and make sure you weren't letting this wealth business go to your head, but I can see you're still in total denial. If you're really convinced the Stryx are going to ask for the money back, my only advice is that you don't start giving hand-outs to whoever calls you with a sob story or you'll end up poorer than you started."

"Thanks, Mom," Kelly replied, thinking that it wasn't such bad advice. "We're having a post-auction party so I really have to go now."

"Give my love to Dorothy and Joe," her mother replied. "And tell those auctioneers they can sell my stuff anytime. Half of the people left on Earth watched your auction, they were calling it 'treasure porn.' The Stryx must have made the feed free because competing networks were broadcasting it at the same time. Some chains even started showing it in immersive theatres for people who wanted the full auction experience."

"Bye, Mom," Kelly replied gloomily and rubbed her belly. So half of Earth's population had seen her mistake a Frunge scratching his head for a bid. I'm never leaving the station again, she said to herself. Alright, I can make an exception for Kasil to try to talk them out of planetary suicide, but they don't watch video.

She took another small sip from Joe's beer and tried to refocus on the conversation at the table, but everybody was sitting silently and staring at her. Finally, an abashed looking Joe said, "Uh, you were sort of talking out loud at the end there, Kel."

Kelly quickly reviewed the conversation and her face began to glow like a tomato. She had broken herself of constantly subvocing for Dorothy's sake, and now it appeared there was a price to pay for changing habits. "Why didn't you stop me?" she demanded.

"Didn't figure out what was happening quickly enough," Joe admitted. "You're not the only one who's getting older. It was just something about Libby setting us up on a date and you waiting for a hint that the galaxy needs repairs."

"Drat," she muttered, and looked around the table. "My mom says that you guys are big stars on Earth," she addressed the Hadad girls. "She said you can sell her stuff for her anytime."

"Kelly's mom has the right idea," Chastity said, brushing over the ambassador's accidental monologue. "You guys really should start an auction business. If Blythe was here, I'm sure she would already have tried to hire you to start an InstaAuction division for BlyChas, but you don't really need us as middlemen. With the Stryxnet infrastructure and the convention centers on all the stations, you could set up an auction circuit, and you know our Stryx will back you. You're the two most famous auctioneers in the galaxy at the moment, so you may as well take advantage before everybody starts to forget."

"What do you think, Sis?" Brinda asked her older sister. "I thought about trying to cash in by starting a business, but given that every sentient with a brain prefers barter, I didn't think there would be enough local demand. Chastity's idea of setting up a circuit might make it work."

"I didn't want to get your hopes up," Shaina replied. "You know it's not going to all be art and artifacts. We'll probably end up auctioning off a lot of broken-down repossessed spaceships and distressed resort world time-shares for centees on the cred. But the video of you knocking down the Forever Stone that incited the Founding War for two hundred billion creds would make priceless advertising."

"If you need help with video production, we could let you borrow Thomas," Chastity offered. "He does the editing for all the InstaSitter commercials, and he can always use the extra cash. He's saving for a new body."

"Thanks," Shaina replied. "We're going to need a different system than Kelly's auction, though. Everything in the last week was guaranteed by the Stryx, so there was no question about accepting payments in escrow or delivery fraud. Speaking of which, who is going to arrange for delivery?"

Everybody turned to Kelly, who spotted Jeeves hovering at the end of the table out of the corner of her eye.

"How are we going to deliver everything?" she called to Jeeves loudly, just as the dozens of conversations at the picnic hit a momentary lull. Everybody waited to hear the robot's reply.

"Didn't any of you read the ABA?" the Stryx replied in exasperation.

102

"ABA?" Kelly asked, even though she suspected Jeeves was setting her up as the straight-man for a one-liner.

"Auction Bidding Agreement," he explained in a rapid chant that Kelly was surprised she could understand without relying on her implants. "All bidders agree to delivery at the Stryx station of their choice within two cycles. Payments must be received in escrow before delivery location may be requested. All items are guaranteed to be as described in the Kasilian catalog and holograms. Any disputes over the condition or identification of the merchandise will be decided at the sole discretion of the local Stryx librarian. All sales are final."

The whole room burst into applause at his machine-gun delivery of the small print, and Jeeves bobbed in place, the robotic equivalent of taking a bow.

"We already sent a science ship to effect the pick-up at Kasil, and they'll shuttle everything up from the surface and deliver it to the stations for distribution," he concluded in his normal cadence.

Brinda whispered something to Shaina and then addressed the robot.

"Is there any chance you'd be interested in going partners in a new auction business?" she boldly asked Jeeves. "We wouldn't ask you to auction off the odd lots of radiation-damaged food or space salvage clothing, but you could help out with the legal stuff and give the firm instant legitimacy on the stations." Not getting any reaction from the Stryx, she hastily added, "And of course, you could do auctioneering whenever you wanted."

"Sold!" Jeeves thundered, bringing another round of applause, and waking Beowulf from his dreams in time to start the endless hunt for leftovers.

Eleven

"I've never been in a swimming pool before," Aisha admitted to Kelly, as they stood a few paces apart at the shallow end. Dorothy swam energetic laps between them, doing a dog-paddle that Joe had taught her in preparation for Blythe's twentieth birthday party, after temporarily filling an old hull in Mac's Bones waist-high with water rented from the Frunge.

Joe had been relieved to have an excuse to teach his daughter to swim because he was brought up to believe that not doing so was the height of folly. Mary Crick was quick to take him up on his offer to teach her younger children as well. But swimming, or even floating, was not really an essential survival skill on a space station where access to the sole human swimming pool was both limited and expensive.

"And I've never been in an executive club before," Kelly responded. "In fact, I didn't even know this place existed before we got Blythe's invitation."

Blythe had rented out the pool area of the club for her party at a price Kelly couldn't even imagine, since her economic outlook hadn't had time to readjust to her Stryx credit balance. In addition to Donna's and Kelly's families, the guests included a large number of young people who had learned to swim before coming to the station and were friends of Blythe, Paul or Chastity.

Both of the EarthCent employees crouched low in the water, Kelly because she was embarrassed that her old bikini no longer contained her comfortably, and Aisha because the modest one-piece swimsuit Shaina had helped her hunt up in the Shuk was the most revealing garment she had worn in her life. It had taken every ounce of diplomacy Kelly could muster to talk the girl out of sewing legs onto the swimsuit. Even though Aisha's father had taught her rudimentary swimming skills in a muddy river when she was a child, the girl was relieved that Dorothy provided her with an excuse to remain with Kelly at the shallow end.

The kids cavorted at the deep end to show-off, many of them skinny dipping, but Blythe herself wore a stylish swimsuit with detachable skirt and shawl accessories that made her look almost well dressed when she came out of the pool. By the time Dorothy had used up her excess energy for the day, Kelly felt like she had been pickled in hydrogen peroxide, or whatever chemical they were using to keep the water so clear. She handed Dorothy up to Aisha and then clambered out of the pool after them, where they gladly wrapped themselves in the towel-robes provided by the pool attendant. Aisha volunteered to take Dorothy in search of an ice cream in the club area.

"What are you oldsters talking about so seriously?" Kelly asked Donna, as she approached the poolside bar where her best friend was in deep discussion with Joe and Stanley.

"The kids," Donna replied, with a furtive glance to see if anybody else had come up. "It's nice to see Blythe around people her own age for a change. When she's interacting with customers, you'd think she was twenty going on fifty, and I feel more like her half-witted sister than her mother."

"It's not that bad," Stanley reassured his wife. "Since I started working for the girls, I've been surprised at times by just how young their thinking can be. They just don't have the experience to be afraid of anything, which can be a big advantage in business if you have Stryx partners to rescue you from your worst mistakes."

"Do you think she and Paul will tie the knot?" Joe asked, never being one to beat around the bush.

"She's never said anything about it to me, but they're both still young, so give it time," Donna replied, though she didn't sound very confident of the outcome herself.

"And how old were you when you became Mrs. Doogal?" Stanley asked his wife facetiously.

"That's different," Donna protested. "I needed a place to stay, and besides, you're eight years older than me so we averaged higher."

"Weren't you a teenager when you guys married?" Joe asked Donna.

"I was practically twenty," she objected. "Besides, I might have been a little bit pregnant."

"And Kelly might be a little bit rich," Stanley observed by way of comparison, drawing a laugh from Donna and Joe.

Kelly glared at her husband and erstwhile friends, even as the smell of the heavily buttered popcorn from the faux-antique movie theatre popper on the bar triggered a new spell of nausea.

"I'm telling you for once and for all that it's not really my money," Kelly gritted out. "It's just another Stryx set-up, I can feel it in my bones. In a couple weeks, Jeeves will be at my door with a seven trillion Stryx cred bill for something, and I'll be a couple hundred billion short."

"Don't worry," Donna assured her, seeing that Kelly really did look borderline sick. "Even if they garnish your salary, we can always stretch the payment schedule so you aren't working for nothing."

"In the long run, we're all dead," Stanley commented cheerfully. "That's how economists used to justify everything to themselves, though of course, the ones making the decisions had guaranteed government pensions."

"When are we headed back to Kasil?" Joe asked. "You have to feel sorry for those folks, calmly preparing for the end of their world by watching it come. Yet they seemed to love their children and they certainly have big families. I just don't get it."

"I did check with a Kasilian woman about that, whether the priests discouraged them from using birth control," Kelly said. "She looked at me funny and answered that children are always a blessing."

"But in your report you said the population was actually very small," Donna pointed out. "Didn't Dring tell you there were more than a thousand times as many Kasilians back when they started withdrawing from the galaxy?"

"Something doesn't add up," Kelly concurred. "Jeeves told me that the Stryx have already dispatched a science ship to pick up all the auction items, and when I asked him why a science ship, he said because they're big and carry shuttles. But if I know my Stryx, the whole auction was just an excuse for them to send in a science ship to work out a solution to the Darkness business. And they want us to go back next week," she concluded, finally answering

Joe's earlier question. "I invited the Cricks along again, since Mary and the children seemed to enjoy it so much."

"Maybe a shrinking population is what put them off of wealth," Stanley suggested. "What I heard about it second-hand suggests they were pretty acquisitive back in their prime, so even though they blew an incredible fortune fixing up their old world, there was plenty left over. If you imagine a population falling a hundred-fold or more, the cycle of inheritance would load the survivors down with more objects than they could possibly use."

"I hadn't thought of that," Kelly mused, recalling what Aisha had told her about the economics of her village. "Their cottages and other structures all looked solidly built, so they probably don't have a construction industry at all."

"From what I saw, their spare resources go into the telescope industry," Joe contributed. "Fascinating equipment. I wish I could have brought one home, but nobody was selling."

"I thought they had recreated a pre-industrial society," Donna said. "Aren't telescopes kind of high-tech?"

"They have craftsmen who work miracles without electricity," Joe replied. "I have no doubt that those people could build a rocket using waterwheels and draft animals for the machine shop work, but of course, the telescopes are mainly about craftsmanship. They have a lens-grinding guild and a metal-working guild that produce the required parts, but the farmers I spoke with were all quick to point out that they had built at least part of their observatory by themselves."

"All of this to watch their own doom approaching and not do anything about it!" Kelly exploded in frustration. "Did they think that restoring their world to something like its original condition would change the laws of physics and save them? Why, they could have bought a dozen established colony worlds for the money they plowed into a planet that may as well be condemned."

"Their telescopes are an art form," Joe said dreamily, his eyes shut in remembrance. "Picture an ancient mechanical watch, with gear works that look like Kelly's knock-off. Then blow it up to the size of a lifeboat, with mirrors and lenses attached to moving parts all over the place. Dring told me that even before they retreated to Kasil, their personal observatories were the envy of stargazers the galaxy over."

"Lot of good it will do them when they're all dead," Kelly repeated her point for emphasis as she looked down at her dress watch. "And it's not a knock-off, it's a replica."

"Are you in a hurry to get Paul married off?" Donna asked Joe, bringing the conversation back around to the beginning. "I thought he was plenty busy with his lab work and helping out with Mac's Bones. To tell you the truth, sometimes I suspect that Blythe might be a little too wild for Paul, though she does a good job of hiding it. I can't imagine what she gets up to on those business trips of hers."

"If I could do it all over again, I would have married my first wife at twenty," Joe replied, still distracted by his memory of the clockwork telescopes.

"You WHAT?" Kelly demanded. "And where would that have left me?"

"Trophy bride?" Donna suggested, as Joe struggled to pull himself back into the present to face the fire.

"I didn't mean, I meant, I would have married you when I was twenty," Joe explained hastily.

"When you were twenty, I was fifteen," Kelly objected. "They still have laws about that sort of thing on Earth."

"So I would have married you when you were twenty," Joe amended himself.

"Do you have a problem with nineteen?" Donna demanded. "Are you saying there's something wrong with Stanley?"

"Timeout," Stanley declared to Joe's relief. "The kids are coming."

Paul and Blythe arrived at the bar at the same time that Aisha returned with Dorothy, who was obviously of the opinion that her robe was a giant, wearable napkin intended especially for sloppy ice cream eaters.

Kelly nudged Joe and whispered, "I want an ice cream," and he gladly seized the opportunity to flee the scene and get back into his wife's good graces at the same time. Dorothy immediately transferred her formidable abilities to monopolizing Paul's attention, and Blythe drew Aisha off to a quiet side table.

"Thank you for coming," Blythe said to Kelly's assistant. "Actually, I'd been hoping for a chance to talk with you."

"Does it have to do with the asylum status for the runaways InstaSitter has been hiring?" Aisha asked. "I asked about it in the weekly report I filed with EarthCent when Kelly was away, but I haven't heard anything back. Kelly said we'd never get an answer, but that as long as the Stryx grant asylum, it doesn't matter what EarthCent thinks."

"No, this is about Paul," Blythe said without batting an eyebrow. "You like him, don't you?"

Aisha dropped her eyes and her face darkened noticeably. "I don't know him that well," she mumbled.

110

"And besides, I would never think of liking him that way when you two are so obviously, uh, a couple."

"I talked to Libby about it since she knows more about relationships than anybody," Blythe continued as if Aisha hadn't spoken. "She suggested we have a contest for him."

"What?" Aisha squeaked in astonishment. "I mean, I know that Libby has been running a dating service forever and that she matched up Kelly and Joe, but, you asked her about Paul and I?"

"Libby said we should either have a contest or cut him in half," Blythe replied. "I think she was joking about the Biblical solution, but you can never be sure with the Stryx."

"What kind of contest," Aisha asked quietly after a long pause, which told Blythe everything she wanted to know.

"She said we should just agree on something," Blythe replied with false bravado as she wilted inwardly. "Are you good at any games?"

"No, not really," Aisha confessed. "I can dance, though I'm out of practice, and I used to work with my mother sewing in our shop. I can do henna, cook some, and the usual housework, of course."

"I can't do any of those," Blythe replied grimly. "Maybe I can learn to cook, though. Are you in a hurry?"

"In a hurry?" Aisha repeated, thinking this must be the strangest conversation that had ever taken place on Union Station. "I don't even understand why you're doing this."

"Neither do I," Blythe replied, almost angrily. "And that's what has me upset."

Twelve

When Jeeves and Joe set the Nova down at Kasil's ancient spaceport, the farm carts were already waiting at a discrete distance to transport the arrivals to Cathedral. Dorothy and Kevin were the first two down the ramp, followed by Borgia, who raced across the weathered tarmac to greet her Kasilian dog friends. The scene gave the detached EarthCent ambassador an idea.

"What about the dogs?" Kelly asked, holding the High Priest's arm to support the older woman as they shuffled cautiously down the ramp. "Before you cured Becky of her callings, she told me that the visions mainly had to do with the natural cycle of your world. You treasure the migrations of wildlife, the renewal of the forests, the cycle of life. Those dogs look pretty happy to me. Has anybody asked them if they want to get eaten up by a giant hole in space?"

"It's not a hole, my dear," Yeafah replied, patting Kelly's hand. "And we celebrate the complete cycle of life, not just the births."

"Let's accept for the moment that you speak for all Kasilians," Kelly began, a line that sounded to Joe like it came from one of her old novels dramatizing courtroom events. "Let's accept that this whole consensus thing is real, and that at least since the time of the Prophet Nabay, your people have had the ability to know when they were

112

of one accord. But are the dogs and the fish and the birds all part of your consensus? Do you only value them as part of some planetary aesthetic, as a proof that you have restored your world?"

The High Priest came to an abrupt halt at the bottom of the ramp and studied the special ambassador's face. For a moment Kelly was afraid that she had finally made Yeafah really angry, and that the old Kasilian was going to blind her with the inner light she possessed in abundance. But as it turned out, Yeafah was simply taking another long look at the aura that Kelly didn't even know she possessed before the trip to Kasil.

"I wish I knew how the Stryx picked people for jobs," the High Priest finally said with a sigh, as she started walking towards the wagons. "The hardest part of my office has always been finding and promoting the priests who do the actual work. It's easy to test their ability in math and astronomical observations, and the aura tells the story of the heart, but how do you measure whether somebody will make the right decisions or say the right things?"

"Are you trying to change the subject?" Kelly asked suspiciously.

"I'm trying to compliment both you and the Stryx," Yeafah replied patiently. "While I assure you that we don't view the cycle of life as some sort of performance art, it does seem that in our quest for transcendence, we may have overlooked some important variables. The synod scheduled to coincide with my return from Union Station will be the perfect opportunity to bring up your point and announce my resignation."

"You can't resign," Kelly protested loudly. "You have to negotiate saving your planet with me!"

"I have already carried out the will of one great consensus for my people," Yeafah replied. "It's time to give a new leader a chance, hopefully one who won't make as many mistakes as I have."

"A Grand Competition?" asked Dring, who was waiting for them as they approached the second wagon. The first conveyance, carrying the Crick family and Dorothy, had already set off towards the forest road.

"It is the only way to select a High Priest," Yeafah confirmed. "If the synod approves immediately, it could take place in twenty days."

"I can't wait twenty days," Kelly objected. "I'm co-hosting a conference next week to establish new regulations for the local ice-harvesting industry. My intern isn't ready for that sort of responsibility yet, and I didn't even brief her."

"The competition itself takes at least another five days," the High Priest informed her. "It depends on whether there is full agreement on one candidate or whether a further trial is required. But the extra time will give me a chance to look into the issues you have just raised. I don't have a strong gift for communicating with the other species myself, but some of our people have the ability to conduct limited discussions with the great birds who aid us with long distance transportation, the long-lived sea creatures, and some of the forest dwellers."

"And the dogs?" Joe asked hopefully, as he boosted first the High Priest and then Kelly into the cart.

"Even I can tell what a dog is thinking," the High Priest replied with a smile. "The challenge is getting them to consider a subject other than food, chasing things that might turn out to be food, or protecting those who feed them. Of course, I don't believe our dogs would choose to leave us under any circumstance. It's not in their nature."

"Why would the dogs leave you?" Kelly asked. "The idea is for you to leave and bring the dogs with you, along with the rest of your planet's life as well."

"What an interesting mind you have," Yeafah observed with a dry chuckle. "I thought you were trying to convince me that we are selfishly ignoring the creatures of Kasil who aren't part of our consensus. But now it appears you are arguing that in addition to not having the right to decide their fates, we must also make our own destiny subservient to theirs."

"Isn't that what you've been doing for the last ten millennia in any case?" Kelly countered. "Haven't you made yourselves into model stewards of the land? Maybe your people were acting out of a different kind of selfishness, a sort of quest for species retirement, or maybe you were doing penance. The important thing is that having done it, you have a responsibility to continue."

"Dogs are tricky," Joe warned, speaking from experience. "If you don't watch out, they'll have you waiting on them hand and foot."

"I recall a legend about a species where an individual who saves the life of another becomes a slave in all but name," Yeafah replied thoughtfully. "They believed that anybody who interfered with the fate of another individual must accept responsibility for the outcome. Since a dead person has no needs and a live person has many, it becomes the duty of the savior to provide for all of the needs of the one who would have left it all behind. I believe this philosophy led to a highly dysfunctional medical system."

"Where's Jeeves?" Kelly asked, looking around as the wagon entered the forest. "He should know about this competition thing as soon as possible. The rest of us should return to Union Station and come back again next month."

"Jeeves flew off as soon as we landed," Joe informed her. "Probably wanted to check on Metoo. If we were anywhere else I could take us back to the station myself, but the tunnel is still restricted access, so we need Jeeves along. I'd love to spend a long vacation here sometime, but it wouldn't be fair to Paul to stick him with running Mac's Bones for a month without even warning him ahead of time."

"If it's acceptable to the synod, I will remain on Kasil until after the inauguration of the new High Priest," Dring said. "I have never witnessed a Grand Competition, and perhaps I can be useful in facilitating communications with some of your less forthcoming species as well. I have quite a bit of experience in this area."

"I've seen him talk with insect things," Kelly seconded Dring's claim. "And trees, he's really good with trees."

"Of course you are welcome Ancient One," Yeafah replied. "It goes without saying. And perhaps your friends with the funny spaceship, the Cricks, would like to remain as well. We owe a special debt to young Becky for starting the process that brought the ultimate resolution to our wealth disposal problem, and all children should spend some time in the fresh air and sunshine."

"I can't give Dorothy up for that long," Kelly immediately told Joe. "We can schedule a longer visit the next time, but I can't go back and leave my daughter with the Cricks for a month. She's only seven."

116

"Of course not," Joe replied. "I wouldn't agree if you wanted to leave her behind, but nobody was suggesting it."

"Oh," Kelly said apologetically. "I guess it's thinking about the children on this planet that brings out my maternal instincts. No offense, Yeafah, but I just don't understand how parents here could raise generation after generation of children with the ultimate goal of giving them to the Darkness."

"It would be difficult to understand for outsiders," the High Priest agreed. "But as I was telling Dring in response to his endless questions about demographics the other day, most Kasilians did choose not to have children. We are much longer lived than humans, so it's only been twenty or so generations since we requested the Stryx to close our tunnel exit, and we've seen negative population growth in all but the last couple generations. Even when I was young, it was still common to see far more old people than children. Now the opposite is true."

"So the closer you come to annihilation the more you want to have children?" Kelly sputtered. "That makes no sense to me!"

"Survival is a natural instinct among all biological species," Dring answered in the place of the High Priest. "I can think of several explanations for why Kasilians might be driven to increase their numbers at this late date. I strongly believe that it's a hopeful sign."

"I know it may seem unfathomable to somebody in your situation, but my ancestors did not have a high opinion of themselves, or anybody else for that matter," Yeafah said, as she adjusted her position on the unpadded wooden wagon bench. "They believed only in material things, what they could see through their telescopes or hold in their hands. Those who embraced the philosophy of materialism with the greatest force were recognized as our leaders, and if not for the coercion exercised by the Stryx, we might have made war on the entire galaxy in our drive to acquire more."

"I don't want to sound disrespectful, but you and your people don't seem anything like your description of your ancestors to me," Kelly said, even as she felt a sudden wave of nausea from the swaying of the wagon.

"Thanks to the teachings of the Prophet Nabay," the High Priest acknowledged, moving her right hand in clockwise circles over her head in honor of his name. "He taught us how to use the consensus to work together towards a unified goal, the very goal you now wish us to abandon. He established the rules for the competitions to select new priests, and the Grand Competition to select his own successor and future High Priests."

"I understand that the tests consist of a series of mathematical and cosmological problems," Dring interjected. "What I don't understand is how you draw them up for each new competition. Surely you can't recycle the same questions over and over again for thousands of years."

"It's a point of honor among us that nobody works on Nabay's challenge problems outside of the competitions. I was elected High Priest without solving any of the challenges in the allotted time," Yeafah replied. "But everybody agreed that I got further along towards solutions than any of the other candidates. After becoming High Priest, I checked the Book of Succession out of curiosity, and it turns out that Nabay himself didn't bother solving the problems."

"Let me get this straight," Kelly said. "You choose the sole leader of your entire civilization based on partial credit?"

"What do you have against partial credit?" asked Jeeves, who had recently developed the habit of soundlessly floating up to people. Kelly called it "sneaking up," but Paul defended his Stryx friend, insisting that it was just a lack of perceptiveness on the part of the humans. "The whole EarthCent recruitment process is built on partial credit."

"Ah, Stryx Jeeves," the High Priest spoke with obvious pleasure. "I was just telling Kelly how much I admire the Stryx system for matching people with jobs. My greatest disappointment during my time in office has been with our administrative failings. For all the effort we put into selecting and promoting priests, I sometimes believe the outcome would be better if I randomly picked farmers off the street on market day."

"The performance of biologicals can be tough to predict," Jeeves agreed sympathetically. "While it's hardly my line of work, I can tell you that the basic Stryx system for finding talent among our fosterlings is to give them ample opportunity to fail upwards."

"What's that supposed to mean?" Kelly asked sourly, expecting to become the butt of yet another of the Stryx's elaborate jokes.

"Think of it as a different form of partial credit, one that awards employees for outcomes rather than for taking a defensible analytical approach," Jeeves answered. "Sufficiently intrusive testing can determine the capacity of a biological to take certain actions or solve certain problems, but capacity doesn't translate directly into results."

119

"I believe Jeeves is saying that they value the right answer over the right reasoning," Dring simplified the convoluted explanation offered by Jeeves. "My own observations of humanity, supplemented by reading from Kelly's library, shows that you assign a great deal of importance to processes and certifications. I believe it's due to your history of working for wages, and your desire to prove your value to employers through achieving quantifiable tasks, even if they fail to bring about an overall solution."

"How else could we have done it?" Joe asked. "I mean, if I got hired to protect a princess of some little kingdom, are you saying I shouldn't get paid if her father loses the war and she can't return home?"

"If Union Station was under attack and you were choosing a guardian to protect Dorothy, would you rather hire somebody who took her away while your home was destroyed, or somebody who protected her by foiling the attack?" Jeeves asked in response.

"But you stated the goal was protecting Dorothy!" Kelly defended her husband. "If you want to hire somebody to protect the whole station, you should say that."

"At the risk of sounding morbid, that's not the way I see it," Jeeves responded, and presented a Kelly-like hypothetical. "Let's accept for the moment that you hire somebody to protect Dorothy, who takes her off the station while it's being destroyed. Then the attackers leave and destroy Earth. So you and Joe and everybody you know are all dead, and some stranger you've hired to protect your daughter has nobody left to return her to, and has to decide whether to adopt her or sell her."

"Well, if you're going to introduce an unknown force that can destroy Union Station into every problem, you may as well just declare every other solution will fall short," Kelly huffed.

"I believe Jeeves is saying that clear-cut problems with simple solutions aren't the real challenge," the High Priest weighed in on the side of Dring and Jeeves. "That's certainly what I've learned through my own management experience. It's easy to find priests who will go where I send them and do exactly what I tell them, but what I really want is priests who will go where they're needed and do what's required without being told."

"They did hire and promote you, Kel," Joe said, suddenly switching sides in what Kelly saw as an act of gross betrayal. "How many special ambassadors do the Styx even employ?"

"Just her," Jeeves replied cheerfully.

"Are you saying that my main qualification is a talent for failing upwards?" Kelly demanded. "Why not say you hired me because I'm lucky."

"Technically, I didn't hire you at all," Jeeves replied. "Gryph chose you for special ambassador because of your track record and availability. If you choose to believe your accomplishments are a matter of luck, I just hope it doesn't run out."

Kelly was still trying to think of a smart reply when another wave of nausea hit her and she threw up over the side of the wagon.

Thirteen

Despite the fact that his research had reached the point where he needed a ship for experiments, Paul felt strangely disappointed when the Nova returned to Union Station a week earlier than expected, with Jeeves and the McAllisters as the only passengers. He and Aisha had fallen back into the habit of having supper together while they had the house to themselves, and they both felt like an invisible barrier had been removed from between them. In an ironic twist, Blythe had started showing up at the embassy every day to have lunch with her mom and Aisha, but had been too busy with business most evenings to go out with Paul.

"I'm glad to see you kept busy while we were gone," Joe said to Paul playfully, after getting back from his morning tour of Mac's Bones and finding his foster son eating breakfast with Dorothy. "Are you trying to create Union Station's biggest ball of junk so we'll have a tourist attraction for the camp grounds?"

"Biggest ball of junk?" Dorothy echoed, her eyes opening wide with excitement. "I want to see!"

"I made it a ball to save space and reduce structural stress," Paul explained. "Any shape would work as a counterweight for a centrifugal acceleration swing."

"If it goes higher than my swing, I want to try it first," Dorothy said, putting in her claim to priority.

It struck Joe that in the absence of both Metoo and Kevin, keeping his daughter entertained when she wasn't in Stryx school could turn into a full-time job for the stay-at-home father. He started mentally reviewing his schedule for the week to see how much of it was kid-friendly. Dorothy always enjoyed watching him work in the brew room and she wasn't bad at measuring ingredients. But he also had a backlog of ship repairs for campers to take care of, and the girl was too young to trust around welding and suspended weights. Then Blythe walked in and Joe remembered that he could always call InstaSitter.

"Your guinea pig is here on time," Blythe announced grimly, though she attempted a smile. She held up a large purple envelope embossed with the name of one of the big passenger liners. "I brought my own sick bag, if you were wondering. Hi, Dot. Hey, Joe. Is this thing going to work or am I going to be getting reacquainted with my breakfast?"

"I was just about to explain it to Dorothy," Paul replied, and began to answer his younger sister's question about the swing height. "It's not a swing like the one on Dring's tree, because it hangs from the Nova on a single cable and it goes all the way around in a circle. Do you remember what you told me about how you feel when you swing?"

Dorothy scowled in concentration, as if being asked to remember something she'd said on a previous occasion was an onerous task. "I was floating when the swing was high and heavy at the bottom."

"That's right," Paul said encouragingly. "At the bottom of the swing, the rope is working hard to keep you from falling as your direction is rapidly changing, and you feel that change in acceleration as being heavier. It's the same idea as the way Union Station gives us weight by spinning."

"I don't believe you," Dorothy replied with a superior air. "Mommy says it's magic. You're just using big words because you don't know."

"I vote for magic too," Blythe concurred, even though like all station children, she had mastered the basic principles of motion in space by her early teens. "But when I travel in smaller spaceships, the ones without enough magic, I get sick. And children who live for months in small spaceships without magic, like Kevin, don't grow up right unless they exercise all the time. Paul wants to fix that."

Dorothy nodded solemnly, accepting Blythe's practical explanation. Paul shrugged helplessly at Joe, who recalled the discussion about finding good employees that the High Priest had started with Kelly after they arrived at the Kasilian spaceport. Maybe the secret to InstaSitter's success was that Blythe saw the universe the same way as the Stryx, favoring serviceable solutions over analytical approaches.

"I built the big magic ball for the Nova to tug into space so it can have something to swing around." Paul tried to adjust his explanation on the fly for his seven-year-old audience. "The idea is that a small spaceship, like the Nova, can start a trip by using fuel to go faster and faster until it reaches its traveling speed. Then it lets out the magic ball on a long cable, and small navigation jets on both the ball and the ship start them swinging around each other, so they both experience magic weight as they coast along together. At the end of the trip, the jets stop the spinning, the Nova hauls the magic ball back in, and then slows down the normal way."

"And because I take after my mother in getting sick so quickly in Zero-G, Paul is using me as a test subject," Blythe added.

"I still don't understand why you went to the trouble of building a mass from scrap, I mean, a magic ball," Joe corrected himself. "Everybody knows that the physics will work, but it's not a practical solution because hauling a magic ball around for a counterweight wastes too much fuel, and fuel is money. Why didn't you just start with using another small ship as the counterweight, since that's closer to your ultimate goal?"

"For one thing, I had extra time on my hands while I was hanging around Mac's Bones in the mornings to handle the camping business," Paul reminded Joe pointedly. "And I'd like to get some practice in before I try to talk somebody into trying it with a real ship. Using navigation jets to spin the ships slowly around a common center of mass when you're already traveling pretty fast gets tricky."

"Can't you start us spinning while the magic ball is still close, and then let the cable out gradually?" Blythe asked.

"If you don't mind the feeling that your head and your feet aren't accelerating at the same rate," Paul reminded her. "That's the reason for a long cable, to move the center of mass, the axis of rotation, as far from the ship as possible, so there's no noticeable difference. Otherwise, you could get the same feeling of weight at any length by just swinging around faster or slower."

"Swinging around the magic ball," Dorothy added knowledgeably as she finished her sugary breakfast cereal.

"Come on, Princess," Joe beckoned to his daughter. "We're going to mix up a big batch of beer, and then we'll

125

go to the Shuk and you can pick out some fruit for flavoring."

"Blueberry!" Dorothy responded enthusiastically, and the two of them headed downstairs to the brew room on the first floor of the converted ice harvester.

"That's one happy little girl," Blythe commented wistfully, after the father and daughter departed. "What do the Stryx have her doing for barter work now that Metoo isn't here?"

"Libby said she'd built up a lot of extra credit since Metoo practically lived with us for two years, so they're letting her slide until it becomes clear whether or not he's returning to school. Since Kelly already spends time reading with her every day, she's way ahead on the basic curriculum, and she only has an in-person class with other kids to do projects twice a week at this age," Paul answered. "So, are you ready to try this?"

"Ready as I'll ever be," Blythe replied, and the two of them headed out to the Nova's berth. Paul had already used the magnetic grapples to rigidly link the ship to the ball of scrap, which had approximately the same mass as the Nova. A few of the campers from Mac's Bones were waiting to watch the strange tandem lift off as they sipped their morning coffees, but the departure was no more interesting than watching a garbage scow in action.

As soon as the Nova cleared the atmosphere retention barrier at the bay doors of Mac's Bones, Gryph took over with field manipulators. The Stryx handled all shipping traffic in Union Station's vast core, spinning up the incoming ships to match speeds with the rotating station, and guiding departing ships to the closer of the cylinder's two open ends. As Paul's ship cleared the station, Gryph gave it a friendly shove in the direction of deep space, away from the tunnel terminal where the vast majority of traffic headed.

"Just hold on another minute," Paul begged Blythe, who was already looking a bit green about the gills. "Do you want me to start deploying the counterweight now, or should I accelerate away from the station to get you some weight back for a bit?"

"There's no point wasting fuel speeding up when you're just going to have to turn around and come back," Blythe answered bravely. "Let the magic ball go and get me some gravity."

Paul shut off the current that aligned the crystals in the tow cable to make it rigid and began paying out cable by releasing the reel brake and backing the Nova away from the ball. In less than a minute, there was a slight bump as the end of the cable was reached, and the ship and the ball immediately began moving back towards one another on the rebound.

"Now comes the tricky part," Paul muttered, as he triggered the preprogrammed navigation jets to start moving the two masses in the opposite direction, parallel to an imaginary point at the middle of the cable. There was a gentle series of bumps as the elasticity of the cable made it act somewhat like a spring. The ship and the ball began to move slowly around the common center of mass.

"I think I feel something," Blythe said hopefully. "Make it go faster."

"They're fighting me," Paul grunted as he tweaked the thrust of the navigation jets by hand. "I estimated the overall elasticity of the system for the calculation, but the error is causing all of these little bumps. This could take a little longer than I thought."

Blythe drew the designer sick-up bag out of the plastic envelope and began breathing into it. "I had oatmeal with yogurt and raisins for breakfast," she warned him between breaths. "This could be pretty gross."

"Don't watch the main screen!" he exclaimed, after looking over to see how Blythe was doing and following her eyes. "Stupid! I should have thought of that," he mumbled to himself, and switched the real-time simulated view of their rotating system to his small navigation monitor. Then he punched up one of the alien nature documentary channels on the main viewer.

"Oh, that's better," Blythe enthused, after a couple of minutes watching the small deer-like creatures with big green eyes nibbling at red fruits that friendly bushes were practically dropping in their mouths. "Everything is much nicer when it's not spinning around."

"We're starting to turn pretty good now, you should weigh around ten pounds or so," Paul informed her.

"Mmmm, better than nothing," she agreed. "So how do you feel about Aisha?"

"What?" Paul choked out in astonishment at the non sequitur. "I'm trying to operate a very complicated system here. Don't surprise me like that."

"Why should you be surprised?" Blythe persisted. "Are you feeling guilty about something?"

"I'm going to try going rigid on the tow cable," Paul replied, pointedly ignoring the question. "If it works, it should eliminate the vibrations."

"You can have as much time as you want to answer," Blythe offered helpfully.

"That's not right," Paul said, dividing his attention between the feedback from the tension sensors and his girlfriend's sneak attack. "Uh oh."

A bank of red lights flashed on the console, followed by a heavy impact on the hull which resulted in a shower of sparks from the main viewer. The lights blinked off, and then came on again with a blue glow, indicating they were running on the emergency batteries. The slight feeling of weight vanished entirely, then came back rapidly until it reached normal gravity as the ship accelerated.

"We're not losing any air, so if the hull was punctured it self-sealed," Paul reported tersely. "I hit the emergency return just in case. Gryph can grab us and take our speed down gently if there's nothing else wrong. I'll come back and try to chase down the magic junk ball after I've checked the damage. Sparks are never a good sign."

"What happened?" Blythe asked sympathetically, even though she was secretly relieved that the experiment was over.

"Cable broke," Paul explained. "Joe's not going to be happy if I don't find the ball and get the magnetic grapples back. The vector of one of the navigation jets must have been a little off, so when I went rigid with the cable, it couldn't take the angular moment. The cable's only strength is in tension when it's extended that far and rigid. When it broke, that cut off the current, so it went from being a long rod back into being a stretched cable and snapped back on us."

"Are you sure you didn't wreck your own experiment to get out of answering my question?" Blythe asked teasingly. "Or does the mere mention of her name get you so excited that you can't fly straight."

"Cut it out," Paul said angrily, still upset over the failure of his maneuver and the damage to the ship. But the instant he saw the expression of forced cheerfulness on Blythe's face crumple into a hurt look, he reached across

129

the central console and grabbed her hand from the armrest. "I'm sorry," he said to the back of her head as she turned away from him. "I'm not mad at you, it's just the experiment—no, it's not that either. I'm mad at myself for being so confused."

Blythe struggled to compose herself before turning back to the young man, who was truly shocked to see wet tracks below her eyes that looked suspiciously like they had been left behind by tears. In the eight years Paul had known Blythe, since he was thirteen and she was twelve, he had never seen her cry. If she had asked him to run away with her and never return to Union Station at that moment, he would have agreed.

"You're my best friend," Blythe finally said, her voice breaking a little with emotion. "I thought that we would always be together so I really didn't think about it at all. Do you know what I mean?"

"Yeah," Paul confessed. "I guess I always just figured you'd tell me what to think when I needed to know."

Blythe tightly gripped the hand that was holding hers, and brought around her other hand in a roundhouse punch to hit Paul hard on the shoulder.

"What's that supposed to mean?" she demanded. Paul saw the corners of her mouth twitching as she fought to restrain a grin, so he knew she was on the way back to her old self. "Am I supposed to be some kind of dictator or something?"

"It just means that I'd trust you with my life," he replied solemnly, looking her squarely in the eye.

"That's not fair!" Blythe retorted, letting go of his hand and rapidly considering her options. "Are you making me responsible for your happiness? Mom always said that men are trickier than they look, but I never believed her until now."

"I'm not trying to be tricky," Paul replied, with one eye on his small navigation monitor as they rapidly approached the station. "I just don't know what you want. I want you to be happy."

"And Aisha?" Blythe asked softly.

"I want her to be happy too," Paul admitted miserably.

"And you?" Blythe prodded.

"I just want you both to be happy," Paul answered after a pause.

"Tricky," Blythe summed up his responses and nodded her head to herself. "Just tell me one thing. What is it about Aisha that's captured you so quickly?"

"I'm not sure," Paul replied. "Even though she has a family back on Earth, there's something of the orphan about her that makes me want to take care of her. Maybe if I was older and she was younger, I could adopt her the way Joe adopted me."

"I need taking care of too sometimes," Blythe insisted.

"Really?" Paul asked in surprise.

"Oh, I don't know," she replied in irritation. "I think you're both tricky."

Fourteen

A group of around two dozen professional treasure hunters and wealthy auction attendees had taken over half of the Mac's Bones campground with their family-sized cabin cruisers. Joe saw it as a mixed blessing, for while they paid cash on the barrelhead, they complained about the hook-ups, the ambiance and the neighbors. He could have forgiven the whining if they hadn't all preferred imported wine to homebrewed beer.

The only thing keeping the unusual campers at Mac's Bones was that they had all won items in the Kasilian auction and chosen Union Station for their delivery point. It didn't take Joe long to figure out that they believed Union Station would be the first stop for the treasure-laden Stryx science vessel, and that would give them a chance to resell their auction bargains before the galactic market was flooded with an influx of high-end items.

Despite their seemingly glamorous occupation, all but one of the moneyed campers turned out to be crashing bores with a talent for calculating percentages. The exception was an ex-mercenary named Clive Oxford, though it later turned out that he had chosen his last name earlier in the month from a brand label in an upscale clothing boutique. Clive looked to be in his late twenties, with a triangular scar on his chin that made it look like he had been shot in the face with a war arrow. Orphaned as a small boy in what might have been a space accident or a failed piracy attack, he told Joe he wasn't sure about his exact age. He had been rescued from starvation by a Vergallian trader and had grown up with no human contact until he was in his teens.

Joe enjoyed practicing his Vergallian on the younger man, and their common background as soldiers of fortune gave them plenty of stories to share over Joe's homebrew. Clive had wised up to the limited career options available to young men fighting other people's wars at a much earlier age than Joe, and he was pursuing a new career as a treasure hunter. Joe politely refrained from asking him how he came to own such a well-equipped scout ship. Beowulf also demonstrated an uncharacteristic liking for Clive from the moment the human arrived in Mac's Bones, and even skipped a nap one time to supervise the treasure hunter's calisthenics outside of his ship. Both men were on their third pint of the evening, though Beowulf was the only one counting.

"The trader who took me in was named Keeto, and he wasn't a bad man for a Vergallian," Clive told Joe in answer to the latter's cautious questioning. "He fed me well and didn't ask me to work any harder than he did himself. I might still be with him today if our engine core hadn't cracked just as we were putting in to Hwoult Three for an overhaul. I was maybe sixteen by then, big for my age, and one of the local man-eaters took a fancy to me."

"Uh oh," Joe interjected, having had his own run-ins with Vergallian alpha-females.

"Yeah, and at that age, I didn't have a clue what was going on. We'd had a bad run of trading and scavenging, I'll tell you more about that in a minute, and Keeto was hard up for cash. The lady, Adree was her name, basically ran the port city, and she made it clear that Keeto could either accept a free overhaul and go on his way leaving me behind, or he would never get off the planet again. I don't think anything scared Keeto more than being stuck on one rock for the rest of his days, and I'm not sure what he could have done even if he was willing to put his life at stake. Anyway, I went to sleep in my bunk one night and woke up in Adree's harem."

"Damn Vergallians," Joe muttered under his breath, but he didn't expand on the point because he wanted to hear the rest of the story. Beowulf was also listening, with his massive head cocked to favor his good ear.

"She was a bit of a tease, Adree, or maybe she was playing a cat-and-mouse game, because she didn't try to dose me with those pheromones right way. By the end of the first morning, I saw enough of her other toys to know I didn't want to become one of them, no matter what. Then I remembered Keeto had warned me before we landed that there was a human mercenary hiring hall on Hwoult Three, and that if I stumbled across them, I might find myself pressed into service."

"You know that's just a Vergallian myth," Joe remarked. "He probably saw one of those Grenouthian documentaries about the old Earth navies and got confused. Either that or he was afraid you'd run off."

"Volunteer or draftee, either of them sounded pretty good to me at the moment," Clive replied. "And sometimes I wonder if Keeto saw the whole thing coming and was making sure I had a chance for an out. Anyway, when Adree sent for me in the afternoon, we both found out that I was tougher than I looked. After a few weeks of hiding like a rat in the under-city and licking my wounds, I found a mercenary crew leaving the system and signed up. I wouldn't have made it without the Vergallian dogs, they used to bring me scraps of food and warn me of the Queen's patrols."

"Makes my life sound like a walk in the park," Joe commented, looking at Clive with new respect. Beowulf offered up a silent atta-boy for the unnamed Vergallian dogs. "How about another beer?"

"Twist my arm," Clive responded, so Joe took the young man's mug and turned to his right to fill it from the tap, all without rising from his seat. The two men and the dog were drinking on the lower deck of the converted ice harvester, which Joe had repurposed as a brew room. Beowulf, perhaps inspired by Clive's story, disappeared upstairs for a moment and came back with a bag of mini-pretzels, which he dropped in the young man's lap. Clive fumbled opening the vacuum-sealed bag, maybe he had never handled one before, and a fountain of pretzels sprayed into the air. Beowulf selflessly assigned himself to clean-up detail.

"So what were you saying about a bad run of scavenging before you put into the Hwoult system for repairs?" Joe resumed the conversation.

"Right." Clive gulped down a handful of pretzels and took a long pull from his freshly drawn beer before continuing his narrative. "The thing about Keeto is that he really wasn't much of a trader, even for a Vergallian. And he didn't care, as long as he could keep his ship flying. His real passion was hunting ancient treasure, though he wasn't above dropping everything and heading for the latest gold-rush, whatever the metal or mineral. Which was good for me, because even though mining is treacherous work, we did more of it on planetary surfaces than asteroids. So I got in a lot of gravity while I was growing, some of it well above Earth normal."

"By treasure hunting, do you mean looking for old wrecks in space to scavenge?" Joe followed up. "I've heard stories about a few aliens striking it rich that way, but it seems to me that it's always from an accidental find, a navigation error taking a trader off the main shipping lanes, or a badly calculated jump coming out the wrong place."

"No, Keeto was a pretty bookish guy," Clive replied. "He told me he would have stayed on Vergal and spent his life studying history if he hadn't needed to work for a living. I've never met an alien who knew so many dead languages because he claimed that reading things in translation just isn't the same. He would spend most of his time on the ship sitting like a statue, reading through whatever historical records he could load onto his heads-up display in search of clues to extinct civilizations. Next thing I knew, we would find ourselves decked out in environmental suits trudging over some wasteland of a world, looking for lost cities. And you know what? We found a few over the years, but they were always stripped nearly bare of anything worth taking and selling, not that Keeto was ever disappointed. It was as much about seeing history first-hand as it was about making a living to him."

"And you caught the bug yourself?" Joe inquired sympathetically.

"I want to find something that no living man has seen before," Clive admitted, a little awkwardly. "It's not that I don't care about galactic history, and I guess I learned something about it from the old Vergallian's conversation. But putting down on some rock that had its atmosphere ripped away hundreds of millions of years ago and looking for traces of an underground city, it's in my blood."

"Not all civilizations end with a catastrophic war or a planetary scale disaster," Joe commented philosophically. "I was on a rescue mission to a planet behind the Mengoth lines around twenty years ago, some place that showed up on the nav console as a number code since it didn't even have a name. No signs of technology or advanced civilization, but the land masses were covered in dense jungle like you wouldn't believe. We landed on the ship's transponder beacon, it was a scout that had gone down after colliding with space junk the moment it came out of a jump, and the vegetation had practically covered the ship less than a month after it crashed."

"Did you get your people back?" the younger man asked, as he draped a hand over the dog's back and scratched behind Beowulf's ears.

"Yes. Although the stuff growing on that world was poison to humans, there was plenty of water they could sterilize and the emergency dehydrated rations held them over. The point is, the crew had nothing else to do while they waited for rescue or starvation, so they took turns exploring. And practically within shouting distance of their crash site, what looked like a small vine-covered mountain turned out to be an ancient city made of some kind of glass substance that the vegetation couldn't crack. They were systematically searching for an entrance when we showed up, and I swear, you never saw people less excited over being rescued. If it wasn't for their rations running low and the possibility that the Mengoths had spotted our ship entering the system, I think we would have needed to use force to pry them away. For all I know, they may have gone back later."

"That's exactly what it's like!" Clive declared, giving Beowulf a friendly thump on the side. "There's something about discovering an ancient structure that makes you crazy to look inside. That's why I'm here," he added, watching Joe closely, as if he expected to read something from the older man's face.

"Maybe there are some ancient locked doors on Union Station, but even if you find any, it's not very likely the Stryx will let you open them," Joe said doubtfully.

"Oh, it's not the secrets of the Stryx I'm after," Clive replied with a laugh, seeing that Joe was totally in the dark about his real quest. "And I see they are as good as their word about keeping the confidence of strangers, even from their friends. I came here because it's rumored that the Kasilians have the last known Key of Eff."

"Isn't that a musical thing?" Joe asked. "It doesn't sound like something you can run out of."

"It's a captain's key," the young man explained excitedly. His eyes bright with fervor, he leaned towards Joe and lowered his voice as if he was worried somebody might be listening. "You've heard of the Effterii, haven't you?"

"Can't say that I have," Joe admitted complacently.

"The legends say that they were the Stryx before the Stryx existed," Clive expounded. "Of course, nobody has records going back that far, not even the Stryx, so much of what I know is from hints and passing references in ancient epics or inscriptions. Keeto made the Effterii his life's work, he would trade everything of value we had on board for the slightest bit of information, even if the source was dubious. I started discussing it with the librarian on the last Stryx station I visited and got referred to Libby, who told me to come here. One of the things that everybody agrees on is that there was a live Key of Eff in the imperial museum of Thark at one time, but the whole collection was lost during their civil war. I believe it ended up in Kasilian hands."

"Must be a valuable thing," Joe observed. "Did it come up in the auction?"

"No, which was almost a relief because I never could have won it in open bidding. But the real reason I'm sitting here waiting is that Libby told me you have a Maker staying here, and he's a historian no less. She said he'll almost certainly be willing to talk to me when he gets back from Kasil, and if anybody can help me find the Key, it's him."

"Other than being old, what makes the Key so valuable?" Joe inquired. When Clive hesitated in his answer, the owner of Mac's Bones added in his old command voice, "I don't figure you as a crook, but if you don't have the money to buy it, what good will it do you to locate the thing?"

"Fair enough," Clive mumbled to himself before answering. "I figure I can strike a bargain with whoever owns the key because I'm the only one who knows where there's a lock it will open."

Joe barked a short laugh and slapped the younger man on the knee. "I guess Keeto didn't raise any fools. So you know where there's an old, uh, Effterii ruin with a locked door, and you need to have a look inside."

"It's not a ruin," Clive answered with a sly grin. "The Effterii were integrated with their ships, which were unlike anything we've seen. Even the Stryx found their technology puzzling when they first came into contact. But according to Libby, they were doomed by their design, a failsafe put in by their creators that eliminated any desire for independent action. She said the first generation Stryx tried to help the remaining Effterii remake themselves, since their creators were gone. But it wasn't a flaw that could be corrected, anymore than humans not being telepathic or not having wings is a flaw. The Effterii's self-awareness is just of a different order than that of the AI we know. They can solve complex problems and maintain the technology that was used to create them, but they basically hibernate unless assigned tasks by a captain. And the captain needs a key."

"So these ships outlived their creators, and then they just shut themselves down?"

"According to Libby, they respond to whoever holds the key, but that made them dangerous, since they contained tremendous knowledge and had limited concerns about its usage. They weren't exactly slave ships, more like a special case of AI idiot savants, but this predates the tunnel network that the Stryx used to basically impose peace on their portion of the galaxy. The leading empires of the time worried that one of their number could exploit the new knowledge to alter the balance of power, so they made a temporary truce to hunt down the Effterii and destroy them. It wasn't that difficult since the ships didn't bother to hide or attempt to protect themselves."

"But you found one," Joe stated.

"Beginner's luck," Clive admitted cheerfully. "When I took my Caged Bird out on a shakedown cruise, I asked the ship controller for a random jump and almost crashed into a rogue planet. It was just coasting through a nebula, a million light years from anywhere, though it looked like it had been through a bombardment from space. My guess is that it was an outer planet from a system that had an encounter with a stray star or a black hole, and after taking a beating, it got caught in a gravity slingshot and was thrown off into space on its own."

"And the Effterii ship was parked in orbit?"

"Nope. Since this dark wreck of a world was the first thing I'd ever found all on my own, I went in for a closer look. One of the deep craters showed the presence of a faint energy field, and rather than getting out of there like a smart boy, I risked a landing and hunted down the source. Most beautiful ship I ever saw in my life, just sitting there and gleaming like the day construction was completed. Took me forever to locate the door, seams were microscopic even on the excursion suit viewer, but the keyhole was obvious."

"Joe?" Kelly called from upstairs. "Are you hiding in the basement drinking beer again? Come on up here, I need you for something."

"You better beat it out the emergency exit," Joe told his drinking companion, pointing towards the ramp he used to roll full kegs out of the brew room. "When she sounds like that, it means her feet are tired and she's looking for a masseur."

"Thanks," Clive replied with a grin. He stooped low to leave through the barrel door and said over his shoulder, "At least you're doing it because you want to and not because she's some Vergallian witch who's stolen your will with pheromones."

"She claims foot rubs are in the marriage contract, but I don't rank high enough to see it," Joe replied. Then he turned and headed up the stairs.

Fifteen

Kelly worried that the all-species ice harvesting conference she had worked so hard to put together was going off the rails. On the final day, a guest speaker took to the podium and began to pontificate, in synchronization with a holographic slide show, on the theme, "What is water?"

"Thank you, Sir Thripaldorp of Pluge," she cut him off, after a new slide contrasting a clear sheet of ice with a pane of window glass appeared. At least, that's what the subtitles suggested, as both the glass and the ice, if they truly appeared in the hologram, were perfectly invisible. "I'm sure we would all benefit from hearing the rest of your presentation and I'll be happy to include a video in the post-conference package if you can provide one. However, we really need to move forward with presenting the treaty to limit interstellar ice harvesting before all the water is used up and our descendents suffer a horrible death from dehydration."

"That was rather dramatic," whispered Ambassador Bork, who sat next to Kelly at the executive table on the stage. "You strike me as rather on edge these last few days."

"Sorry," she muttered back. Sir Thripaldorp slunk away from the lectern to be replaced by Ambassador Czeros, who was carrying a watering can in one hand. Kelly suppressed a groan and looked away, as without a word, the Frunge diplomat began to water his own head. "It's this stupid symbol of office. If I had known the conference president had to wear a big flat rock as a necklace, I would have let somebody else do it."

"The rock symbolizes the absence of water," Bork assured her. "It's been worn by the presidents of ice treaty conferences for millions of years, as witnessed by the number of marks commemorating treaty signings."

"It's crushing my chest," she complained, then immediately grew embarrassed. Kelly was proud of the close working relationship she maintained with the Drazen ambassador, but he didn't need to hear about her breasts being sore. "Is Czeros drunk again? He promised me he'd dry out for the conference."

"He did," Bork informed her in amusement. "He's just showing off now. See how there isn't any water dripping on the floor?"

Kelly gave her full attention to the ambassador's performance, and realized that the vine-like garden of his hair was capturing all of the water and turning a vibrant green before their eyes.

"Yuck, that's kind of gross," she said, without understanding why she should feel that way, since the Frunge descent from trees was no secret. The watering can empty, Czeros flung it aside, bowed, and took his place with the other ambassadors at the end of the Kelly's table. She glanced at her interactive speakers list, and found that the next three presenters had scratched themselves at some point in the last few minutes, almost certainly as a result of her treatment of Sir Windbag from Pluge. Oops, that made it her turn. She rose from her seat and approached the lectern.

"My fellow concerned species," she began, then paused to shift the heavy slab that hung around her neck and felt like it was preventing her lungs from expanding fully. "I won't bore you with philosophy or put you to sleep with statistics, since we've all had enough of that already. The question at hand is one of the long-term survival of biologicals in the sector. Those of us fortunate enough to live on a Stryx station, with their highly efficient water recovery system, would be largely unaffected by the increasing scarcity of harvestable ice in the local space. But those of you who are building new orbitals or trying to terraform lifeless worlds will find that the expense of bringing water from distant volumes of interstellar space will be prohibitive."

Kelly paused for a moment to catch her breath and wondered why she felt so out of it. Becoming introspective in the middle of public appearances was something new to her, and she speculated that the weight of being a Stryx cred trillionaire was getting under her skin. Yet, that very morning she had argued with Joe over calling an InstaSitter for Dorothy while he and Paul made repairs to the Nova. Five creds an hour to babysit an angelic seven-year-old struck her as extortionate. In a better galaxy, she was sure people would be lined up to pay for the privilege of spending quality time with her daughter. In fact, that might be a good idea for a business...

"Stryx to Kelly," Libby spoke over her implant. "You're delivering a speech, in case you've forgotten."

"Oh, sorry," Kelly jerked her head up and wondered how many of the assembled diplomats had noticed her wool gathering. No, don't think about that, she told herself. Just give the speech.

"While interstellar ice is a slowly renewing resource through supernovae and interstellar winds, the giant factory dipole trawlers deployed by some of the species present are rapidly denuding certain volumes of space of commercially significant supplies," Kelly read from her heads-up display. "The treaty will limit ice harvesting in any cubic light year of space to one thousandth of one percent of the proven reserves per year. While this limit will undoubtedly prove painful for those who have invested heavily in harvesting infrastructure, this committee believes it is necessary to guarantee the viability of space dwelling for future generations."

"One thousandth of one percent!" shouted an angry Frunge from the assembly. "At a tenth of a percent we'd have a struggle to make payments on our ships."

"This committee has proposed as the first amendment to the treaty a provision for extending no-interest loans to equipment owners, and in extreme cases, may authorize buying the equipment for scrap or resale in another sector," Kelly replied calmly.

"We don't want to go out of business," boomed a fast-spoken Verlock in a voice like rolling thunder. "You may as well declare commercial ice harvesting illegal as impose those limits." A loud chorus of ship owners howled their agreement.

"Friends, fellow species," Kelly shouted above the clamor, surprising herself with her own passion. "There's something greater at stake here than your businesses. Interstellar space is the common well from which we all dip, and it's not right that some take so much more than they need to sell it for wasteful industrial processes and open-cycle commercial space farming. The marks on this heavy stone around my neck witness how many times this treaty has been implemented in the past, only to be gradually forgotten as civilizations rise and fall and hyper-efficient harvesting equipment is reinvented."

"Who are you to tell us what to do," cried one of the few human captains from the open admissions gallery. "I've raised my family on an ice harvester and they all know how to do an honest day's work. But you, you could buy out every ice-harvesting outfit here with your pocket change and still have enough left for a beer. Stop messing with our lives and go back to your robot friends."

"You know what?" Kelly said, wiping the carefully prepared list of talking points off of her heads-up display as the applause for the heckler died down. "I'm beginning to wonder if any of you guys even read the conference package before you registered. The treaty was the first item included, and after the speaker schedule, lunch menus and advertisements from our sponsors, we included another copy of the treaty with non-technical explanations of each and every clause that a ten-year-old could understand."

"One thousandth of one percent means that at the maximum harvest rate, it would take a hundred thousand years to use up the local ice crystals!" called the same Frunge who had initially interrupted Kelly's planned remarks.

"So what's your point?" she asked roughly, giving the alien her toughest stare.

"You humans were still drinking out of your hands a hundred thousand years ago, and you hadn't figured out how to dig a simple well, much less keep it separate from your outdoor latrines," the Frunge continued to the obvious enjoyment of his fellows. For the umpteenth time since moving to Union Station, Kelly wished that anthropological documentaries of the up-and-coming species weren't one of the most popular entertainments on the galactic networks. "You haven't even been bathing for a hundred thousand years, and you're trying to tell us about water usage?"

"Do you know why there's enough water out here for you to keep that sorry patch of weeds you call hair from drying out?" Kelly shouted in response, and poked dramatically at the newest groove on the oversized stone pendant suspended from her sore neck. "Because forty-two thousand years ago, your ancestors signed this very same treaty. And here, ninety-six thousand years ago, they signed the one before that. And here, and here, and here, all the way back to when your forebears were competing with the grasses for dominance on the plains of your home world! Don't talk to me about a hundred thousand years being a long time. I've got two million years right here crushing my nipples!"

The crowd noise was evenly split between angry shouts and laughter as Kelly panted with emotion and tried to catch her breath for the next round. She glanced at the executive table to check on her supporters. Czeros was leaning over to conceal his head behind the bulky Verlock ambassador and draining a hip flask. Bork had a hand over his mouth and his tentacle was wrapped over his eyes, a sure sign of Drazen embarrassment. The Vergallian ambassador favored the EarthCent ambassador with a warm smile, setting off alarm bells in Kelly's head that she must be making a fool of herself. Aisha materialized at her elbow.

"Ambassador?" Aisha whispered in her ear, leading Kelly to speculate that her intern was checking to see if her superior had been possessed by an evil spirit. "Are you feeling alright? Donna and I were worried that you don't seem to be yourself."

Kelly looked out over the crowd to the door of the conference hall, where Donna was fulfilling her usual duties as registrar. Her friend gave an encouraging wave, and then placed her hands together like she was saying a prayer, lifted them to her shoulder and tilted her head down towards them. Kelly interpreted the pantomime to mean that the embassy office manager thought the ambassador wasn't getting enough sleep. Which was true, in part because of all of the cracker crumbs she had created in bed last night after a midnight attempt to settle her stomach, but there was hardly anything she could do about it at the moment.

"I'm fine, Aisha," Kelly whispered back. "Why don't you take my seat at the table while I wrap things up, and please try to get Bork to come out of hiding. It's rather childish, don't you think?"

"Yes, Ambassador," Aisha responded, though Kelly wasn't sure whether she was agreeing about the Drazen ambassador or just acknowledging her instructions. In any case, their brief conversation gave the attendees a chance to calm down, so Kelly could make herself heard without shouting.

"I'm sorry, I really am," she began again in a conciliatory tone. "It happens that I live in the crew quarters of a scrapped ice harvester myself. But there are more interests represented here than the ice fleet captains, industrial water users and equipment manufacturers. Nobody is accusing you of any wrongdoing, and we all want to implement this treaty with the least amount of economic dislocation possible."

"But we weren't even invited to the negotiations," complained an artificial person with metallic skin who must have been the representative of a manufacturing orbital. "What's so sacred about one thousandth of one percent? Interstellar winds have changed since the treaty was first written, and our own data suggest that the ice crystal density in local space has actually been rising for the last few years."

"Thank you for your question," Kelly answered sincerely, since she had prepared a response for this one. "The terms of the treaty are identical to the terms of similar agreements throughout the galaxy, dating back to the Founding Wars, and they are written to promote political stability as well as to preserve water resources. Such agreements are so fundamental to the coexistence of species that reopening them to negotiation carries far more risk than any possible benefit. I know that's not an answer you want to hear, but it represents the collective wisdom of sentient creatures stretching back to a time before most of us existed."

"Well, it sucks," the artificial person responded, drawing a fresh round of supportive applause. "What you're telling me is that you held a three-day conference to deliver the bad news. I blew my vacation time on a bunch of presentations about water conservation in manufacturing processes put on by eggheads who have never set foot on an orbital. I could have stayed home on Chintoo and given my fuel cell a rest."

"The conference package made it clear that the treaty was already ratified," Kelly repeated. "I'm sorry if you didn't learn anything of value from our conference, but we really did our best. I personally participated in the selection process for the sessions, and if there had been any presentations submitted from Chintoo or the other local orbitals, I would certainly have given them full consideration. But as it happens, all of the interest in presenting at the educational sessions was from academics and salesmen. I really am sorry."

Something hot and wet was running down Kelly's face, and she looked up to see if it was dripping from the ceiling. The audience was strangely silent, which was a relief, though she thought her voice had sounded a bit funny at the end there. Probably the weight hanging around her neck taking its toll. She felt an overwhelming urge to sit down on the floor, but as she began to do so, a strong arm circled her waist and prevented her.

"Let's take a break for a while," Ambassador Bork suggested soothingly, as he led her back to her seat. Kelly wondered why Aisha wasn't in her chair, but then she realized the girl was walking on her other side, supporting her by the elbow. "Just let the stone rest on the tabletop, nobody will be offended."

"I'm so embarrassed," Kelly mumbled in reply, repressing a strange urge to continue crying. "I can't tell you what's come over me."

"You'll tell us when you're ready," Bork reassured her. "Do I have your permission to wrap up this conference so we can all go home and rest?"

"Yes, please," Kelly replied, surprised at the relief she felt when Aisha settled into Bork's vacant seat to keep her company. She tried to remember if the instant coffee she drank at the office that morning could have been a white-labeled depressant cup that got mixed in with her regular coffee. That's the only thing she could think of to explain her sudden mood swings.

"Before we conclude the conference and initiate galactic broadcast of the signing ceremony that has already taken place," Bork put a special stress on the last four words, "I'd like to remind any of you who are looking for work that the Belugian consortium is hiring experienced crews for comet-mining operations in the sector."

A groan from the audience showed that they were familiar with the difficulty of the work and the rock-bottom wages and bonuses non-stakeholders could expect to be paid. All of a sudden, accepting a buyout from the treaty commission didn't sound so bad, which was exactly the point Bork wanted to make.

"I'd like to thank my fellow ambassadors for their efforts in planning this event, especially Kelly McAllister of EarthCent, who volunteered to carry the stone forward despite the thanklessness of the job. If there are any immortal species in the audience, let me take this opportunity to invite you back for the next conference in fifty thousand years or so. Thank you, come again."

Bork raised both hands in the Drazen gesture that indicated he was done talking, and the ensuing cacophony of folding chairs scraping the floor gave witness to the fact that everybody got the message and was heading home.

Sixteen

Blythe and Aisha met on the ag deck, where Donna's
girls had gotten their start in business by taking flowers on
consignment from the nurseries and selling them in the
café district at night. The fields were separated by a
network of paths that disappeared into the ceiling with the
gradual curvature of the deck. Both girls wore shorts and
had just come from purchasing rubber soled shoes at the
Shuk, after realizing that they only owned high heels,
sandals, and in Aisha's case, dancing slippers.

"So you should have an advantage, being a dancer and
all," Blythe told Aisha, after explaining the proposed route
for the race. "I don't really do any regular exercise on the
station since work keeps me so busy."

"Could you tell me again why we're doing this?" Aisha
asked. "I thought we were becoming friends. Can't we
settle this some other way?"

"Do you want to share him?" Blythe inquired in
response, watching Aisha's features closely. "I didn't think
so. Libby did point out that neither the Stryx nor the
majority of the aliens on the station have any problem with
plural marriages, but I don't think I could do it myself."

"But he hasn't ever said anything to me about it," Aisha
protested. "How do you know he wants to marry either of
us, or anybody for that matter?"

"It'll be one of us, I've decided that already," Blythe informed the diplomatic intern. "He's my best friend, and I'm not about to allow him to marry just anybody."

"I really don't understand you," Aisha replied with a sigh. She sat on the grass and changed from her sandals into the cheap sneakers. "How is running in a circle going to change anything?"

"I don't know," her new friend admitted glumly. "But I've known Libby my whole life. She handles most of the teaching for the Stryx school in her spare time, you know, and we've been in business together for years. If Libby says we should have a contest for who gets Paul, then there must be a point to it."

"Are you sure the paths all connect the way you described?" Aisha asked, conceding defeat for the time being. The reality was that she could only stand up to Blythe when Paul was around. Otherwise, the sheer force of the young tycoon's confidence made her question herself for doubting the wisdom of anything Blythe said.

"Chastity and I used to come here and walk the same route when we had to talk over tough business choices," Blythe told her. "It was a bit over a half an hour, but we would walk pretty slow when talking, so it shouldn't take long running. Besides, the gravity here is a little lower than on the residential decks, though of course, living with Kelly on the docking deck, it probably feels normal to you. So are you ready?"

"Not really," Aisha admitted, stretching to touch her toes.

"Then, GO!" Blythe shouted, and took off running before the startled girl could recover. For three or four minutes the girls ran up the gently curving deck at break-neck speed. Blythe felt her breath coming harder and

153

louder with each inhalation, but she refused to slacken her pace or look behind her. Aisha might have been in better overall shape, but older girls were discouraged from running in her home town because it wasn't considered decent once they began approaching womanhood. She did her best to keep up with Blythe, but before she knew what hit her, Aisha had a stitch in her side that felt like it was tearing her flesh apart. She staggered to a halt.

"Wait!" Aisha called to Blythe in one explosive exhalation, before bending over and pressing a hand under her ribcage. She couldn't look up to see whether or not the other girl had heard, so she didn't know Blythe had in fact stopped running until she felt a hand on her back.

"Are - you - hurt?" Blythe panted out the question, wondering if she had broken Kelly's intern. "The oxygen level - is usually higher - on the ag decks. Maybe we started - out too fast."

"We?" Aisha replied with a grimace as she tried to rub out the cramp in her side. She decided against trying to straighten up, instead sitting down with an uncharacteristically clumsy thud. "If I'm dying, you're going to have to hire somebody to help Kelly," she added accusingly.

"You'll be fine," Blythe assured her. "I really thought you'd beat me - without a problem. Dorothy said you could dance for hours."

"Then why did you insist on racing?" Aisha asked her. "Why not a contest you thought you would win? I would have agreed to anything, you know."

"I know, and that's exactly the problem," Blythe told her. Receiving a puzzled look from her rival, she attempted to explain. "In business, there's always competition. Even when I was a little girl selling flowers,

154

there were people who saw how much money we were making and tried to do the same thing. Chastity and I never hesitated a moment to do whatever it took to beat the competition. We even spent our savings selling at a loss for a while to protect our turf."

"You won today too," Aisha told her. "I'm the one sitting on the floor."

"No, the contest was first one to the finish," Blythe replied. "I've had enough of this for today. I'm taking you out for a meal to apologize when you can get up. Let's call it a draw."

"You still haven't explained why you seem to want to lose to me," Aisha insisted, holding out a hand for Blythe to help her up.

"I don't want to lose to you, I just don't want to beat you either," the other girl admitted. "I guess this was one of Libby's dumber ideas."

"Dumber ideas?" Aisha asked in shock, looking around as if she expected the wrath of the Stryx to descend on Blythe's head. "It's probably just that we don't understand."

"You didn't grow up with Stryx the way station kids do," Blythe countered. "The Stryx seem to know everything because, well, they sort of do know everything, but that's not the same as understanding what's inside somebody's head. When we go to Infinite Snow Cones for dessert, do you think Libby could guess what flavor you're going to order?"

"Probably," Aisha confessed, knowing that she always became intimidated by the hundreds of thousands of syrup choices from around the galaxy and ordered the mango-flavored ice every time. But now that she thought about it, the three times she had gone there with Blythe after lunch, the other girl had ordered a different flavor every time, apparently picking at random. "But I'll bet she couldn't guess which one you'd choose."

"Why did you join EarthCent?" Blythe asked suddenly, as if she just figured something out. "I mean, I know they contacted you out of the blue with a job offer, that's how they hire everybody. But why did you accept?"

"I wanted to help people, to make a difference," Aisha replied after thinking for a moment. "It was really scary. I didn't know if my parents would disown me or if I would ever be able to see them or my sisters again. But I knew it was the only chance I would get to leave my village and do something big. And the truth is, I was never happy at home and I didn't think it would ever get better. So I guess I really did it for myself."

"Do you want to become an ambassador?" Blythe continued her line of questioning. "Do you plan on staying with EarthCent until you're an old lady, or would you do something else?"

"I haven't really thought that far ahead," Aisha admitted. "I know that a lot of the other diplomacy candidates in the orientation course had their whole career plotted out, but I just wanted to get started. I can't believe how lucky I've been, coming here as Kelly's intern. But would I want to be in charge of an embassy, or sent on a mission to try to talk a whole alien civilization out of suicide? I don't think so. I was never any good at getting my little sisters to do their chores, and I can't imagine trying to tell grown men how to act."

"I can," Blythe replied firmly. "If Gryph asked me to take over running Union Station tomorrow, I'd ask him what time I start. I love being in charge. It's one of the reasons I turned down EarthCent when they offered me a starting post a few years ago. No matter how high you go, you never really get to run anything. It's all government with the consent of the governed under the supervision of the Stryx."

"I didn't know anybody turned them down," Aisha said in a hushed tone, looking at the older girl in wonder. "You really are serious about running things, aren't you?"

Blythe remained silent for a moment as they reached the little pile of sandals and bags they'd left by the path ten minutes earlier. Nobody had disturbed their things, in fact, nobody had even come by or they would have noticed, but all public areas of the station were under constant monitoring in any case. While there was crime on Stryx stations, it took the form of cheating on contracts or the unpredictable crimes of passion. Of course, most activities that were illegal on Earth weren't crimes on the station in any case, though the Stryx wouldn't interfere with species that enforced their home culture's rules for their own citizens on their exclusive decks.

"I don't want to tell Paul what to do," Blythe said finally. "I'd never know if he loved me or if I was just good at managing him."

"I understand," Aisha replied, wondering if she could ever be so strong herself. "You do love him after all. I was hoping you just wanted to keep him out of habit."

"Did you know he got started on his artificial gravity research because I complained about getting space sick all the time?" Blythe asked the other girl as they headed back towards the lift tube. "He gets mad when I call it artificial gravity though, he says there isn't any such thing. But I don't care whether it's gravity or acceleration that keeps my feet stuck to the floor and the food in my stomach as long as it works."

"He mentioned at breakfast that they were almost finished with the repairs from the first failed experiment," Aisha replied, and immediately felt guilty for pointing out that she lived with the object of their mutual affection. "I don't really understand what he's trying to do. Surely all of the ways of spinning ships around in space have been known for a very long time."

"Paul likes proving to himself that things work, rather than accepting everything he reads," Blythe explained, taking some comfort in the fact that she knew so much more about him than Aisha. "He wanted to start with a simple counterweight, then try it with two ships, and finally, to design a new type of small vessel for humans that can separate into two pieces once it reaches cruising speed. With a long cable between the two halves, a slow spin could give the occupants enough weight to keep their bone mass and stay healthier on long trips. It's really all about ship design rather than physics."

"Is he doing a, uh," Aisha paused as she fished for the unfamiliar word. "I'm sorry, I forgot what you call it when somebody gets an advanced university degree. Nobody in my family has gone beyond the teacher bot education."

"A dissertation," Blythe supplied the word. "No, the Open University run by the Stryx doesn't have a formal graduate school like they do on Earth. You can get certificates for achieving occupational competency, like Laurel, who used to live in your room, got accredited as a multi-species chef by the culinary college. But in general, people go to the Open University to study something they're interested in. It's not like Earth where you need a degree to get a job doing something. All of the employers I know on the station, human and alien, will let anybody take their job entry tests."

"So he goes to the Open University to study ship design, and some day he's going to want to move to an orbital factory for work?" Aisha asked.

"Take us to Paul," Blythe commanded, as they entered the lift tube. After the door closed and the capsule began to accelerate smoothly, she returned to Aisha's question. "No, I don't think so. If his design ideas work, he might start building custom ships in Mac's Bones, but I don't picture him ever going to work for somebody else. What's the point of that? If he needed to make money, he could go back to professional gaming. I know he still plays Nova with Jeeves at least once a week, and that's probably enough to keep him competitive."

"He was a professional gamer?" Aisha asked in surprise. "But I thought he was our age, maybe one or two years older."

"Paul became a Nova grandmaster before he turned eighteen," Blythe told her proudly. "That's how he bought Joe the tug for Mac's Bones. And he was the last surviving commander of the Earth fleet in the largest Raider/Trader battle. We could have won too, if Chastity and Tinka hadn't killed everybody," she added ruefully.

"You're so lucky to have known him so long," Aisha said enviously.

"We've been best friends since I was twelve and he was thirteen. Joe came to Parents Day and talked about their junkyard dog, so I visited Mac's Bones afterwards to see Beowulf. But I was really just curious to see where Paul lived because he seemed so nice and shy. Then Joe and Kelly got married, and with my mom and Kelly being best friends, we practically became family."

"I never had a best friend," Aisha admitted sadly.

"This is what makes the competition so unfair," Blythe said in mock anger, just before they turned into the corridor where Paul's lab was located. "How could anybody not like you?"

Seventeen

"This first one looks really nice," Donna said over Kelly's shoulder, as the women studied the slowly rotating hologram of an attractive planet that floated above the ambassador's display desk. "But you have to be careful. Stanley claims that a good real estate photographer can make a garbage dump look like a botanical garden."

"Where's the price?" Aisha asked from Kelly's other side. "I want to keep track of all of the vital statistics so we'll have a way to compare the candidate worlds."

"The prices are on the audio feed," Kelly replied. "I asked Libby to mute it because the sales pitches made me feel pressured, but maybe that's just because I was viewing them alone. Libby? Can you turn the sound back on please?"

"Just say 'play' or 'pause' to control the audio," Libby announced. "I just hope you don't set your heart on any of these worlds before you return to Kasil next week."

"Why is that?" Kelly asked sardonically. "You keep telling me that it's my money and I can spend it any way I want."

"That's true," Libby replied smoothly. "But it's obvious that you're shopping for a planet to give the Kasilians, and if you do succeed in convincing them to move, I think it would be better to let them participate in the selection process."

"First of all, I was thinking of buying one and renting it to them as a business," Kelly stated, though her declaration lacked conviction. "Second of all, I haven't been very impressed with their decision-making to this point."

"Play," Donna interjected, putting an end to the theoretical discussion and bringing them back to the serious business of window-shopping.

"Furlon Six. Paradise at a price you can afford," the voiceover began. "Are you a nitrogen/oxygen breather? Is your world overcrowded or facing imminent destruction? Do you just need a place to get away from it all? Make Furlon Six your dream planet, all for the unbelievably low price of two trillion Stryx creds. Let's take a closer look, shall we?"

The holographic image zoomed through fluffy white clouds, making the viewers feel like they were flying above the surface and coming in for a landing. Lush vegetation rushed at them, causing all three women to lean backwards. Next came picture-perfect white beaches and blue lagoons surrounded by coconut palms.

"Freeze image!" Donna cried, and stepped nearer to the hologram for a close look. "Isn't that a picnic table under those coconut palms?"

"What's that thing that looks like a sign?" Kelly added. "Libby, can you zoom in on it, next to the driftwood?"

"The Caribbean Islands Tourist Council asks you to deposit your litter in the marked receptacles," Aisha read from the blown-up sign. "But who would go all the way to Earth to steal a no-littering sign?"

"I think the realtor may be taking liberties with some stock footage," Kelly told her intern gently. The girl turned dark with embarrassment at her own naiveté.

"Libby? Do you have any current imagery of Furlon Six?" Donna asked.

"Just a sec," the station librarian replied. The hologram wavered for a moment, before being replaced by a strange-looking green and blue planet that resembled a show-and-tell project Dorothy had made for her first Kindergarten project a couple of years earlier. Then the image zoomed in and all three women narrowed their eyes in disgust. It looked like somebody had strip-mined the entire surface of the planet, and then covered it with colored foam to try to make it look livable from space.

"That's awful," Kelly cried, the very sight bringing on a sudden feeling of sadness, accompanied by nausea. "Make it go away, Libby. Isn't that criminal misrepresentation or something?"

"The Furlon system isn't on the tunnel network, but even if it was, real estate has always been a 'caveat emptor' business," Libby responded. "The green foam appears to be a standard terraforming seed and micro-organism mix, so as long as the surface minerals aren't toxic and the oceans still produce precipitation over the land masses, the planet could end up with a reasonable base of topsoil in a few thousand years."

"Is that what Kasil looked like when the Kasilians started going home?" Aisha asked out of curiosity.

The hologram wavered again, and the image of a pockmarked planet bedecked with an infinite number of lights appeared. As it rotated, a jagged gap in the connected super-cities came into view, along with multiple space elevator tethers along the edges.

"This is what Kasil looked like at the beginning of their clean-up process," Libby informed them. "It never looked like Furlon because the Kasilians stripped the metal skin in

163

patches and replanted as they went. The whole process only took a few hundred years since the Kasilians had more than enough barter items to convince the contractors to work overtime. There are still plenty of partially metal-clad worlds in the galaxy if you want to see one. I'm sure that nice young man who's helping Paul with his ship-design experiments could tell you all about the abandoned ones. He's quite a treasure hunter."

"Clive?" Kelly asked. "The guy who gives the vibe of being a professional bodyguard or something? I know that he gets along well with Joe and Paul, and even Beowulf likes him, but I wouldn't have thought to characterize him as a nice young man."

"He sounds interesting," Donna said, and winked at Kelly. "What do you think of him, Aisha?"

"I don't know, he seems older I guess," replied the girl, who only had eyes for one man at a time. "Are we giving up on planet shopping already?"

"No, and I don't have a clue how we got on this subject," Kelly answered. "Could we have the next planet, Libby?"

A hologram of a mountainous world replaced the image of Kasil hovering over Kelly's desk, and the voiceover began immediately.

"Cedthi-Gruhl. Where your future and past come together. The unspoiled Northern hemisphere is ideal for your agrarian dream home, while the industrialized Southern hemisphere provides a steady income stream. This cash-flow-positive planet is available by special offer for the price of just four point seven trillion Stryx creds, and includes a defensible perimeter around the desirable residential areas of the North. The current planetary overlords are selling due to estate planning reasons, and have transport in place to evacuate on short notice. Visit Cedthi-Gruhl. Seeing is believing."

"It's occupied and they're fighting a war?" Kelly asked incredulously. "Who would buy a planet like that?"

"Maybe the overlords of a different planet without a defensible perimeter," Donna suggested, being well-versed in strategic military affairs from attending twenty years of gaming trade shows with her husband. "Doesn't look right for the Kasilians, though."

"Could you maybe only show us the worlds that the Kasilians might like?" Aisha asked Libby hesitantly.

"Certainly," the Stryx responded. "Just remember that I'm not endorsing the purchase of any particular world nor suggesting that the Kasilians be compelled to evacuate their own planet."

"You sound more like a lawyer every time we talk," Kelly complained as she conceded the point. "Alright, please show us the real estate the Kasilians might consider calling home if they should mysteriously agree to changing their minds about going softly into the dark night."

The hologram of Cedthi-Gruhl blinked out and was replaced by a three-by-three grid showing nine globes of roughly the same diameter, but rotating at various speeds about different axial tilts. They all showed areas of blue, green, white and tan, and some included large patches of red as well. Libby had helpfully added a few vital statistics under each, and presented her own summary of the offerings.

"These are the top nine candidates within a reasonable distance of Kasil that are either on the market or welcome mass immigration. Starting with Brank Four at your top left, it's been a factory-farm world for the last several hundred thousand years, so there's no question about title. The main drawback, from the Kasilian perspective, is that the natural cycles of this world were disrupted long ago, and even the weather is controlled by satellite. But the seller does offer to pick up the cost of reasonable alterations to rotation rate, etc. They would probably accept a five-trillion cred offer because their production and shipping costs have rendered their products non-competitive with some of the newer factory-farm worlds and closed-cycle space plantations."

Aisha scribbled furiously on her screentab with a finger as the other two women watched Brank Four turn through a full cycle.

"It looks nice from space," Donna commented. "And there must be an advantage in dealing with businessmen rather than empires or tyrants."

"Well put," Libby agreed. "The next world, GY73R, is currently unoccupied by any life forms that we would recognize as sentient, though it's always possible to miss something, especially in the oceans. It was once part of the Brupt Empire, but they left the galaxy to pursue their aggressive expansion outside of the Stryx sphere of influence. It's currently owned by the Vergallian Empire..."

"Next!" Kelly interrupted.

"Are you going to refuse to buy a planet from every species that ever made a pass at your husband?" Donna inquired.

"I'd rather buy a planet from the Gems," Kelly replied.

"Funny you should say that," Libby continued calmly. "Our next planet belongs to the Gems and was also a factory-farm, but they no longer need it since their nutritional needs are being completely met by a drink

166

synthesized from industrial byproducts. However, the native flora and fauna have long since been replaced by cloned varieties of..."

"Next," Aisha said, and then covered her own mouth with her hand in horror of having interrupted Libby. Kelly and Donna both turned to look at the intern, who defended her reaction in a much less authoritative tone. "You weren't at the fundraiser for the ag deck the Gem gave up. Nobody would want to live on a Gem farm world unless you killed everything and replanted."

"Now Brindle is a lovely world, one I visited as a young Stryx during my ambulatory phase," Libby continued. "The gravity is a little higher than Kasil because the planetary core contains more iron, and the Brindles themselves are a very friendly and accommodating species who are looking to sell settlement rights to the unused continent in the Eastern sea. The main drawback from the standpoint of the Kasilians might be the rotational speed, which leads to a day that is nearly four times longer than the cycle on Kasil."

"Why are they selling settlement rights to a continent?" Kelly asked suspiciously.

"Well, they believe it to be haunted, and in a sense it is," Libby admitted. "But that's unlikely to bother the Kasilians, who are a very spiritual people and would probably get along fine with unsettled dead who, of course, aren't even their relations."

"Are you pulling our legs, Libby?" Donna asked.

"If you don't believe in ghosts, just ask young Clive," Libby replied. "Anybody who's visited enough ruins will tell you that something of the builders always remains behind."

"Have you signed up as his public relations agent or something?" Kelly asked. "And what's the story with the big red splotches on that pretty planet with the beautiful white polar caps?"

"Brupt Prime is still a bit of a rehab project," Libby admitted. "The Brupt sort of destroyed it when they left, their own version of a scorched-earth strategy, though who they meant to deprive of its resources isn't clear. In any case, that was a long time ago, and our science ships occasionally visit to push along the natural decontamination process. It's currently quite safe for a species like the Kasilians, whose version of DNA employs a redundant error correction scheme. The red patches are deserts created by metal-eating bacteria the Brupt developed as a weapon, but it's long since died out for lack of comestibles. It does mean the Kasilians would have to import any metal needed for their farm implements and telescopes, but they don't use that much."

"If these are the cream of the crop, I'm beginning to suspect that there aren't that many prime residential planets for sale," Kelly observed.

"It's not so strange if the native populations have anything to say about it," Donna replied. "How about the planet next to it with the smaller red spots."

"Brupt Minor," Libby reported. "Same star system, same basic story, a little colder in the winter and hotter in the summer. The main drawback here is that at the apogee of its orbit, it passes through the fringes of the asteroid belt that used to be Brupt Major, resulting in spectacular meteor showers and the occasional dinger."

"Dinger?" Aisha asked.

"I think she means an asteroid that makes it to the ground without burning up and impacts with the force of advanced weaponry," Kelly explained.

"Yes, but a relatively simple asteroid defense system can completely solve that problem," Libby countered. "And the planets themselves are unclaimed, so there aren't any other costs involved, other than the ongoing clean-up and bombardment defenses."

"Even with the problems, how could the planets go unclaimed for so long?" Aisha asked.

"There were some rumors about booby-traps, but surely most of them would have aged out by this time," Libby brushed past the subject quickly. "Now, the next world is new on the market. It's a complete terraforming job done on spec by a consortium of Horten and Dollnick construction clans. It will support anything imported from Kasil, and naming rights go to the purchaser. While the workmanship is impeccable, the Kasilians may be uncomfortable with the fact that it was a lifeless ball of rock for billions of years before the engineers went to work on it."

"The next one looks promising," Kelly said, feeling strangely moved by its beauty. "It sort of reminds me of Earth."

"Isn't that the Great Wall of China?" Donna asked, as the globe spun before them.

"Oh, there's India!" Aisha declared.

"It's just an idea I'm throwing out there," Libby said cautiously. "Most of your large nations could fit the remaining Kasilian population in a corner where nobody would notice them. They could be the next Pennsylvania Dutch."

"I don't think Earth is ready for an influx of forty-million or so alien astronomer-farmers," Kelly replied doubtfully. "But I haven't been back for over twenty years, so what do I know? I'll send a query off to EarthCent, or better yet, I'll ask my mom. At least that way I'll get an answer."

"Well, I saved the two most logical options for last. Both of them are former Kasilian colonies. The one in the middle of the bottom row is Setti Five, where Becky Crick went through her religious phase. The current population largely consists of descendents of the guest workers, and in some instances, slaves, of the original Kasilian colonists. While they are spread over the globe, the total population is less than a billion, so there's more than enough room to absorb the Kasilians. Any lingering hard feelings could likely be plastered over by a sufficiently large donation to the Setti Five Benevolent Association."

"What about the one that's almost all blue?" Aisha asked.

"New Kasil," Libby replied. "It was the first colony the Kasilians founded when they began exploring interstellar space, and they primarily used it as a resort world. A group of Dollnick contractors took it in barter for rehab work done to Kasil and they've run it as a resort world ever since. There aren't any true continents, just some very long island chains, and while it would support the Kasilian population with no problems, many of their native species would be out of luck. And it isn't officially on the market, but with the Dollnicks, you know it's just a matter of price."

"Is that really it?" Kelly asked. "Nine choices in the whole galaxy? I thought there would at least be hundreds."

"I'm only displaying worlds that aren't too far from Kasil, where the ownership isn't in question and the Kasilians could be settled with a minimum of fuss," Libby explained. "If they were willing, the better option would be to set out in colony ships and discover a new home. Gryph estimates that of the hundreds of billions of planets in our galaxy, there are still millions of unclaimed worlds that would suit their purposes."

"Gryph wouldn't happen to have picked one out for them already?" Kelly asked warily, reflecting on the lukewarm selling job Libby had done on the nine worlds she had chosen for reasons of her own. The holograms disappeared from above the desk and the station librarian didn't answer.

Eighteen

"Don't care much for Zero-G, do you?" Clive asked, trying to make light of his concern. Jeeves had only cut the power to the Caged Bird's engines a minute earlier, and Blythe was already taking deep breaths with her eyes tightly shut. She had invited Aisha along for Paul's second cable swing experiment without thinking about the fact that the Nova only had two acceleration couches. In a momentary flare-up of self-sacrifice, she offered to go with Clive, who had volunteered his ship as the counterweight to the Nova. Jeeves came along to pilot Clive's scout after the treasure hunter admitted he had never been much for fancy flying.

"I'll be better soon," Blythe replied, though she sounded like she was about three gasps away from launching a mess of partially digested food into the small ship's cabin.

There was a reassuring clunk as the magnetic grapple on the Nova's towline locked onto the nose plate of the Caged Bird, and the two ships began backing away from each other.

"Almost there," Jeeves commented cheerfully.

Blythe's body pulled against the safety harnesses of the command chair, rather than sinking into the cushions as was usual when a ship accelerated forward. Clive looked on in awe as in the space of two seconds, the Stryx pilot hit full reverse thrust, followed by a micro-blast from the main engines to bring them to a dead stop with the towline just going taut. At the same instant, Jeeves fired the auxiliary lateral navigation thrusters that Joe and Paul had temporarily affixed to both hulls that morning.

"Seriously?" Blythe asked, as the centrifugal force made itself felt almost immediately. "It seemed like it took Paul forever to get us started going around the magic ball the last time out."

"It's an old Stryx trick," Jeeves replied modestly. "I could have accelerated us up to the spin rate where you'd feel Earth normal gravity already, but Paul wants to monitor the tension on the cable to create a data set. Besides, I had a selfish motive for getting the job done quickly."

"Showing off to a poor human pilot?" Clive asked.

"I had myself polished for tomorrow's return to Kasil and I happen to know that somebody had spaghetti for lunch," Jeeves replied, as the comm came to life.

"Nova to Caged Bird," Aisha's voice sounded tentative over the link. "Am I doing this right? Paul is busy with his cable measurement and he asked me to check on Blythe."

After waiting a few seconds, Jeeves explained, "You have to say 'over' when you're done talking so we know it's our turn. Blythe is feeling much better. Over."

"Oh, that's good," Aisha replied guiltily, knowing that Blythe hadn't expected to spend her day a full tow-cable length away from Paul. "Uh, Over?"

"If you're done with the conversation, you say 'Over and Out,'" Jeeves informed her. "Over."

"Oh, then, Over and Out for now, I guess," the girl replied.

"Don't," Blythe interrupted Jeeves, before the robot could explain the archaic radio communications protocol further. "Next time just open the main viewer so we can see each other talking like the rest of the intelligent life in the galaxy."

"You two seem to know each other quite well," Clive commented in a friendly manner, maneuvering to enter the conversation. "I know that we were introduced before we boarded, but you seemed a bit distracted. My name's Clive."

"Hi, Clive," Blythe responded, feeling a little ashamed that she really hadn't registered the man's name during their introduction, a serious professional lapse. But this was her day off, after all, and she had expected to spend it showing Paul how she and Aisha compared, which struck her as a pretty dumb idea in retrospect. "I'm Blythe, and this is Jeeves, but I think you knew him already. Jeeves does some work for me from time to time since I'm in a business partnership with the Stryx, and we've known each other forever through the school."

"A business with the Stryx?" Clive asked with undisguised interest. "I never had any direct dealings with Stryx until I stopped into Middle Station to ask their librarian some questions a few weeks ago. I was referred to your station librarian here, and I can't get over how generous she's been with her time. But I never knew the Stryx went into business with humans."

"Sure, just talk like I'm not even here," Jeeves muttered loudly.

"Everybody calls our station librarian Libby," Blythe replied, ignoring Jeeves remark. "I guess a lot of people don't realize that the Stryx use businesses and partnerships to promote galactic stability and regulate the value of the Stryx cred. My sister and I started InstaSitter with the help of Libby, and then we partnered with the older Stryx to franchise across the station network. I'm always traveling between stations to meet with the local managers."

"Must be rough if you can't get used to Zero-G," Clive said sympathetically. "Do you spend all the flights in stasis?"

"No, I hate stasis," Blythe declared with sudden energy. "It's like agreeing to die and then being brought back to life. I just have a couple bad hours after departure, but I usually get my space legs long before the trip is over."

"I've spent so much time in Zero-G that I don't even notice it," Clive admitted. "Of course, I practically live on the exercise equipment, reading from the display or working with the teacher bot."

"Aren't you a bit old for a teacher bot?" Blythe asked with her characteristic bluntness.

"I had a kind of funny childhood," Clive replied, not wanting to sound like he was fishing for sympathy. "I didn't get started working with the teacher bot until I bought this ship, and that was less than two years ago." He registered the surprise mingled with pity on Blythe's face and hastened to add, "I'm not completely ignorant. I spent a lot of time reading when I was a kid, and I know as much about dead alien civilizations as some historians, a lot of it from hands-on expeditions. But I'm kind of behind on math and science."

"I didn't mean it that way," Blythe found herself apologizing. "There's something that makes you look like you've already done more in life than most people."

The main view screen flickered, and the artificially generated view of the two ships rotating around their

175

common center of gravity on the long towline was replaced by the Nova's bridge. Paul was down on one knee next to Aisha and was holding the girl's hand.

"I think I hit the wrong symbol," Aisha said dubiously. "Couldn't you afford voice control for this ship?"

"Of course we have voice control," Paul told her. "But if you're going to be my back-up pilot, it's important to learn to operate on manual controls in an emergency. This gesture pad was actually designed for Verlocks and they only have three fingers, so you have to get used to separating your own fingers in pairs."

A steaming Blythe, an amused Jeeves and a puzzled Clive all watched as Paul manipulated the girl's fingers, pushing the pinkie and ring finger together, squeezing the middle finger with index finger, and then pulling her thumb gently out to the side.

"You see? Just practice a little and you'll be able to run the nav pad as if you were born with three fingers," he declared, still holding her palm with his other hand and beaming at her like a lovesick schoolboy.

Blythe reached over and tapped Jeeves to get his attention, and then slashed her finger across her throat. The Stryx deactivated the main viewer.

"So what is it you do, Clive?" Blythe asked, to cover her embarrassment. If the man realized there was something wrong in the dynamic between the two crews, he didn't show it.

"You could call me a treasure hunter or an amateur alien archeologist, and I'm passionate about it to the point that some people think I'm a little nuts," he said with a disarming smile. "I've been exploring alien ruins from the time I was a little kid, and ever since I got the money

176

together to buy my own ship, I've been on a mission to recover some Effterii artifacts. Have you heard of them?"

"There was something in Stryx school," Blythe replied, searching her memory for details. "They were an early race of artificial intelligence that outlived their creators and spread through space looking for other life. But they had some fatal flaw, right?"

"They weren't so much flawed as different," Clive defended the objects of his obsession. "Are dogs flawed because they aren't wolves? In any case, the biologicals that created them had disappeared for good, and the remaining Effterii either went into service for other aliens or entered a sort of hibernation. Then the biologicals turned against them and wiped them out in the days before Pax Stryxa."

"That's so sad," Blythe said in empathy for the ancient AI. "Did any of them survive?"

"There were always rumors that the ones who went into hibernation were still out there, but finding a medium-sized ship that's gone dark in interstellar space is like searching for a particular atom on a planet," Clive replied, though he wasn't really sure about the mathematical accuracy of the comparison. Between a sudden urge to impress the girl and a surprising inability to contain his own enthusiasm, he added the proud declaration, "I found one."

"An ancient AI that predates the Stryx? Is it still alive? Are you listening to this Jeeves?" Blythe fired the questions in rapid order.

"It was alive enough to prevent me from getting in without a key," Clive responded. He unconsciously massaged the hand that he had momentarily feared was frozen solid by the Effterii defensive shield when he touched its hull, despite the armored spacesuit he'd been wearing.

"The Stryx are aware of Clive's quest and we support his goal," Jeeves replied. "Of course, we don't want to interfere directly."

"I came here because there's a chance the Kasilians have a key, and because your librarian, Libby, told me there was a Maker on the station who might be able to help me," Clive repeated the same basic facts he had given Joe. "If I could get back there with the key and get inside, I'd bring the Effterii to Union Station for the Stryx to examine. The Effterii were supposed to use a jump technology that's completely different from what we currently use, allowing them to jump from within strong gravitational fields."

"Does that mean we could travel without having to spend so much time in Zero-G?" Blythe asked excitedly. "If that's the case, I'll back you if you need funds."

"You really must hate weightlessness a lot," Clive replied with a laugh. "I know less about how jump drives work than the average school kid, but I'm sure Jeeves could explain to you why the Stryx do things the way they do."

"Biologicals get themselves into trouble when travel becomes too quick and easy," Jeeves stated flatly. "The minimum trip time we'll facilitate through the tunnel network is a little over two human days, point to point. Ships traveling greater distances are intentionally slowed in proportion to allow biologicals time to adjust. While I wouldn't say you all act alike, there's something in biological brains that tracks at least a sub-conscious approximation of absolute position, and ignoring it can lead to violent outbursts, especially for biologicals traveling in large groups."

"How come I don't remember this from school?" Blythe asked skeptically.

"I seem to recall somebody deciding she knew everything and dropping out early," Jeeves retorted.

"Well, I know I hate being weightless," Blythe said, unfazed by the robot's accusation. "And I must have spent nearly forty days in space last year, just traveling between stations. The only positive thing about it was I got to catch up on all the sports gambling I couldn't do at home without shocking my mom."

"I've never bet on sporting events myself." Clive struggled to restrain the smile twitching at the corners of his mouth. "I'm told that it's too easy to rig the matches."

Blythe looked at him again, closely for the first time, and he swore he could feel her eyes boring into him.

"Would you be shocked if I told you that I won a bundle on Zero-G cage fighting when I was only seventeen?" Blythe asked, but didn't stop to wait for an answer. "Would you accuse me of being a silly female bettor if I told you I let it ride on a fighter named 'The Masked Mercenary' until he stopped competing?"

"Are we up to Earth normal yet?" Clive asked, turning towards Jeeves. "Feels pretty good to me."

"Isn't it a funny coincidence that The Masked Mercenary was just about your size, and had an identical scar on his chin where the mask didn't reach?" Blythe continued her interrogation-cum-soliloquy. "And I wonder where a poor boy who grew up without a teacher bot would find the money to buy a scout ship and name it the Caged Bird?"

"Look," Clive said suddenly, "I've tried to put all of that behind me, so I guess I shouldn't have gotten so cute with the name of the ship. Other than digging in ruins,

179

fighting was all I was ever good at, and as the youngest guy on a mercenary crew, I got plenty of opportunity to practice. I did the cage rounds for one year to save up money for this ship, and then I got out. Aside from you and the Stryx, nobody knows that Clive Oxford was the Masked Mercenary and I'd like to keep it that way. I didn't like the kind of attention I got as a professional fighter."

"Your wish is my command," Blythe replied, holding up her hands in submission. "Why don't you tell me more about the alien ruins."

Six hours of intense conversation later, the ships returned to Union Station. As Clive and Blythe disembarked through the main port, Jeeves whistled after them in Stryx short code, "Just get a room already." Libby immediately rebuked her offspring for being a bad sport.

Paul and Aisha were all for preparing a late dinner at home for the four of them, but Blythe insisted she had to get back to work. Clive asked to tag along to see the InstaSitter offices, and the two of them walked from Mac's Bones to the nearest lift tube.

"Office," Blythe instructed the lift tube, and the capsule set off smoothly.

"I don't want to sound like a jerk," Clive began tentatively, then he decided to start over. "So are you and Paul a couple?"

"He's been my boyfriend for nearly three years," Blythe answered bleakly.

"He's not very good at it," Clive observed.

The capsule made a sudden dive and a twisting lurch, literally lifting the humans off their feet and throwing them into the same corner. Clive, with his Zero-G cage fighting reactions, maintained body control throughout the maneuver, and with one powerful arm, guided Blythe to a stable landing on her feet.

"I get it, Libby," Blythe said out loud. "You can stop now."

Nineteen

The Grand Competition was in its last scheduled day when Kelly arrived back on Kasil with her family and Jeeves. Shaun and Kevin came out from Cathedral to meet them, driving a borrowed cart, with Borgia and a couple of native Kasilian dogs following behind.

"Mary would have come, but they're putting up preserves today and it's an all-hands-on-board affair," Shaun apologized for his absent wife.

"Seems they could spare the two of you," Joe jested.

"I'm all thumbs in the kitchen, and the boy eats everything that's put down in front of him," Shaun replied. "And how's our young lassie doing?"

Dorothy looked up from the collection of interesting bits of this and that which Kevin had been emptying from his pockets to impress her with the folly of ever returning to Union Station.

"Good, Mr. Crick," she answered. "But nobody calls me a lassie anymore. They call me an heiress."

"We'll see how long that lasts," Kelly muttered under her breath to Joe, who regarded her with amusement. Whether or not she was right about being a cog in some Stryx master plan for saving the Kasilians, it seemed to her husband that she had been infected by the miser bug. During the few weeks of her tenure as one of the fat cats of the galaxy, her personal expenditures had dropped as if

182

she felt the need to save every centee for the future. Joe had even caught her folding up the aluminum foil from a take-out container for some undefined reuse, though she laughed it off and claimed she wasn't even conscious of what she was doing.

"Does this wagon have to sway so much?" Kelly moaned just a few minutes into the ride. "Stop for a moment and let me down so I can walk for a bit."

Shaun reined in the animals, and Joe swung Kelly to the ground and then hopped down beside her. The landing reminded him that he was getting a little too old to be hopping off of anything. After twenty minutes of plodding along and nibbling on the hard biscuits that Mary had included in their picnic lunch provisions, Kelly felt better and got back into the wagon, riding the rest of the way to Cathedral.

By the time they reached the guest quarters, the sun was just starting to set. Shaun and Joe continued on with the animals to the stables after dropping off Kelly, Dorothy and Kevin. The communal canning work had come to an end, and the rest of the Cricks were waiting in the dining hall to greet Kelly and her daughter.

"Where's Dring?" Kelly asked, after catching up on the agrarian accomplishments of all of the Crick children.

"He's off watching the Grand Competition," Mary explained. "He still comes home every night, not that any of us have ever seen him sleeping."

"I do hope they finish on time and appoint a new High Priest who's willing to listen to me," Kelly replied hopefully. "I really came to like Yeafah, but she just wasn't willing to make a decision about abandoning Kasil."

"It's such a lovely place," Becky said sadly. "Since we've been living here, I've come to understand the meaning of the visions I used to receive. It's so hard to believe that all of this will be lost forever."

"It doesn't have to be lost," Kelly responded fiercely, drawing the attention of the entire Crick clan. "Well, at least the way of life they've created here can be saved. It just has to be moved somewhere else."

Joe and Shaun entered the dining room, took their seats, and made rapid inroads on the ample provisions.

"You have to take Dorothy outside to see the show, Kel," Joe announced between bites. "They must have started lighting candles before it got dark, because the whole town is glowing like a fusion core. We almost skipped dinner to stand there and stare, but then we thought we better come in and tell you about it," he concluded with a happy belch. Shaun nodded his agreement, his mouth too full of pie to speak.

"Aren't we blessed to have husbands who always have our best interests at heart," Mary said, with just the right degree of enthusiasm to convey her skepticism.

"Whatever their motivations, they are correct about the spectacle," Jeeves announced from high above the table, causing Shaun to swallow the wrong way when he looked up. "It means the Grand Competition is concluded and a new High Priest has been selected. We are all invited to the coronation, which will take place as soon as the Stars of Nabay appear."

"Come down from there, Jeeves," Kelly demanded irritably. "Can't you just float in at ground level like a normal robot? And how many weeks do we have to wait before the Stars of Nabay appear? I'm beginning to suspect this whole competition was just a Kasilian delaying tactic."

"Where did Gryph find such a moody ambassador?" Jeeves asked nobody in particular. "The Stars of Nabay,

184

which are the most prominent constellation in the Kasilian sky, will be fully visible in approximately sixteen minutes. So if you don't want to miss the coronation, I would suggest less talking and more walking."

Eleven chairs scraped noisily back from the table as the humans all rose and trooped out the door. After a month of living at Cathedral, the Cricks could have found the main assembly hall in the dark, but as Joe had said, the night was lit up by what seemed to be millions of candles in paper lanterns. Kelly and Mary did their best to ride herd on the younger children, but in the end, they were left with just Kevin and Dorothy. Jeeves vanished as suddenly as he had appeared.

The main hall of Cathedral was an enormous room that was already packed with locals and the candidate priests who had attended the Grand Competition. But the humans were met at the entrance by Dring, around whom a polite bubble of space was formed. Dring had corralled the other Crick children as they arrived, and once he had the whole human contingent together as a group, he proceeded to lead them all down the main aisle to the very front of the hall.

Kelly was surprised they were receiving such special treatment, but she knew that the Kasilians venerated Dring, and supposed they had saved a prime pew for the guests. But she was taken aback when Dring led them right up onto the dais and seated them in a row of chairs, one of which was occupied by Yeafah. Dring indicated that Kelly should take the seat next to the outgoing High Priest, after which he went to stand at the end of the row.

"We're very honored that you're making us a part of such a special event for your people," Kelly addressed Yeafah through the voice box in her best diplomatic manner, feeling a little self-conscious in front of the huge crowd of Kasilians. "I hope the children don't create a distraction. It's hard for Dorothy to sit still for very long."

"Don't worry about a thing, dear," Yeafah replied with a smile. "We Kasilians don't stand on ceremony, so it will be over in a few minutes. After all, how long can it take to announce the results of a competition which can only have one winner?"

The question brought back a bittersweet memory of the interminable school awards ceremonies Kelly had suffered through in her childhood, where everybody got a prize for something. She even seemed to recall a particularly dreamy boy in her sixth grade class getting an award for passivity. Of course, the combination of teacher bots and emigration put all schools in the position of having to hunt for students, and handing out boxes of ribbons and certificates to all attendees was a cheap insurance policy. Suddenly Kelly realized that Yeafah was no longer sitting beside her and that the former High Priest had already begun her announcement.

"And it is with great pleasure I can announce that the rumors you have undoubtedly heard are true. The winning priest is the first individual in our history to solve not only one, but the entire set of Nabay's challenge problems, an accomplishment prophesized to initiate the dawn of a new age for our people. So without further ado, I give you the High Priest of Kasil!"

The assembled throng burst into the chant, "High Priest, High Priest," as Metoo floated onto the dais, bobbing to the left and to the right as he came. The little Stryx approached Yeafah, who removed a black stone ring from her own ring finger and stuck it onto the lower jaw of the robot's extended pincer. Metoo bobbed again, then remained alone in front of the multitude as Yeafah returned to her seat and the hall fell quiet.

"Although the Stryx policy is not to interfere in the affairs of sentient species, I am a child whose actions cannot be said to establish legal precedence for our kind," Metoo declared. "Therefore, I will immediately conclude negotiations with Special Ambassador Kelly McAllister for the removal of all Kasilians and whatever other life of this world that can be saved to a new home. Thank you for the interesting math problems. I enjoyed them very much."

Kelly sat stunned as the hall erupted again, this time in chants of "Me-Too, Me-Too." The beaming sea of faces told her that the famously pessimistic Kasilians had, as Dring previously hinted, transformed themselves into a race of optimists. She was still struggling to take in the fact that her daughter's former playmate, admittedly a math whiz by his very nature, had just been chosen as the leader of an entire species, when Dring ushered the humans from the dais into a small backroom that was smoky from too many candles.

"Hi, Dorothy," Metoo said, as soon as the door was closed and the roar of the crowd was muffled. "Did you like my speech? Grandpa Dring helped me with it."

"You're a big hero!" Dorothy exclaimed, and gave the little robot a hug as Kevin looked on sullenly. "Mommy was so worried about the Kasilians, and now you're going to save them all."

"Dring and I have been appointed by Metoo as his advisors to arrange for the Kasilian exodus with the Special Ambassador," Jeeves announced. "The former High Priest has arranged for a musical entertainment to celebrate the inauguration, so if we can wrap up negotiations quickly, Metoo can make the announcement before the visiting priests leave for their trip home."

"That sounds good, huh, Kel?" Joe prompted her, seeing that his wife looked almost as unhappy as the youngest Crick.

"I don't see why you needed me here at all," Kelly replied sulkily. "It seems to me like the Prophet Nabay wrote the entire script ten thousand years ago."

"You have to admire Nabay's solution," Dring chortled "He recognized that his people were in decline, and like many of the older, wealthier species, they had spread themselves thinly among the stars, buying up country manors and private islands with ample supplies of native domestic help. When his observations and mathematical prowess led Nabay to the conclusion that Kasil was doomed, he used his people's innate pessimism to lure them home and dedicate themselves to the seemingly meaningless task of rehabilitating the planet of their birth."

"Do you mean that from the very beginning, his goal wasn't the actual restoration of Kasil but the process?" Kelly asked. "He set out to save his species with partial credit?"

"Exactly," Dring replied, slapping his tail on the floor in admiration. "Nabay knew that his people couldn't change overnight, and that it would take many generations to breed out the pessimism. He needed a way to keep them all in one place so the survivors could still find mates. No true pessimist would ever agree to give away his choicest treasures for the sake of spiritual purity. When the Kasilians reached that consensus almost two months ago, it meant that the last pessimist had died off, and the subsequent move to divest themselves of that wealth was an unmistakable signal to the Stryx that they were ripe for rescue. Nabay was more than a mere prophet. He was able to reach forward and shape the future ten millennia after his death."

"I guess I am being a little selfish," Kelly admitted. "I'm just not used to having the fate of a species hanging over my head, and it's made me a little moody. So what can we do to save these people?"

"Libby told us that you've done some shopping for planets, but for a variety of reasons, we think it would be best if the Kasilians were able to start fresh, on a young world with no baggage," Jeeves explained. "Gryph and the other first generation Stryx have come up with a short list of compatible worlds that never developed sentient life forms. These planets remain unknown to the biologicals of the galaxy, in some cases because we've hidden them away against future need."

"So all that's required now is a fleet of spaceships and shuttles to move forty million odd Kasilians and as much of their flora and fauna that will fit in the ships to one of these worlds on short notice," Kelly reasoned. "Could a Stryx station do the job?"

"A station would work as a fallback for the population, but it would mean disrupting the tunnel network and temporarily putting a hundred million or so station residents out of a home," Jeeves answered. "I'm sure you know that there is a 'higher purpose' eviction clause written into all Stryx station leases, but it's a clause that hasn't been invoked in millions of years."

"Colony ships could do the job," Joe observed. "I saw one years back that held ten million humans and enough of an ecosystem to start fresh on a terraformed world. But I imagine they take a long time to build."

189

"Interestingly enough, the Lorthest Orbital shipyards ceased their commercial ship construction activities a little over a century ago to focus on building a fleet of colony ships," Jeeves informed them innocently. "Of course, that happened before I was alive, so I wasn't around to see what led them to make that decision, but I understand they built the ships on spec, without a customer."

"Quite a risk for them to take," Kelly responded dryly. "I wonder what the going rate is for a fleet of colony ships?"

"I'm told they would accept around six trillion," Jeeves replied. "That would include the fueling and shuttles, of course."

"Of course," Kelly repeated.

"There's no money left in the Kasilian treasury," Metoo reported mournfully, and sank towards the floor. "I've only been High Priest for ten minutes and I'm already a failure."

"Mommy has it!" Dorothy informed her friend, and tugged excitedly at her mother's arm. "Mommy, please give your money to Metoo to save the nice Kasilians."

"You realize this means you can't have a pony," Kelly teased her daughter.

Dorothy stood still for a moment to digest this information, and then she hugged Metoo again. "I never asked for a pony, and you have to help Metoo!"

"Then let me state for the legal record that I will be happy to pay 'around six trillion creds' to the Lorthest Orbital shipyards for a fleet of colony ships," Kelly said. "I authorize Stryx Jeeves to access the auction proceeds account to make the payment, and if there's anything left when it's done, I hope Metoo will accept the money for the Kasilian treasury as a rainy day fund."

Metoo spun around several times in joy, and then headed back out to relay the good news to his followers. Kelly felt like the weight of the world had been removed from her shoulders. Besides, she reflected privately, *the Prophet Nabay isn't the only one who saw this coming, and maybe now my lower back will stop aching.*

Twenty

To help Kelly decompress after their brief trip back to Kasil, Joe arranged for a surprise picnic at Mac's Bones. Metoo remained behind on Kasil until the evacuation could get under way and a new High Priest could be elected, though it wasn't immediately clear how the Grand Competition would be conducted since Metoo had solved all of the challenge problems.

In addition to Donna's family and the Hadad girls, Joe invited Ambassador Bork and his family, along with Clive. The guests had already polished off the barbeque by the time Dring arrived, but the Maker was a vegetarian and probably came late on purpose.

Joe caught Clive's eye across the table when the friendly little dinosaur appeared, and told him, "That's Dring, but give him a chance to eat some celery sticks before you start in with the Effterii questions."

The younger folk all crowded in around one of the end-to-end tables, leaving Kelly and her friends at the other. Clive sat strategically on the seam line, with Blythe to his left at the youth table, and the space he had saved for Dring on his right. Dorothy had adopted a similar strategy, not being able to choose between Paul and her parents, so she sat across from Clive.

Being back home with a full stomach and a fresh glass of beer was finally lightening Kelly's mood, but she still had trouble letting go of the fact that the Stryx had kept her out of the loop on their Kasilian plans until the last second.

"I know everything worked out for the best, and I understand that the older Stryx are trying to walk a thin line with the noninterference philosophy, but it still hurts that you couldn't trust me," Kelly complained to Jeeves. "I never thought I would crack under the pressure of not knowing what was going on, but I haven't been myself ever since that first trip to Kasil."

"I agree with you one hundred percent," Jeeves declared to Kelly's astonishment. "We really should have been more open with you from the start, but instead we caused you unnecessary suffering and misery. You could almost say that we were your, uh, what's the word I'm looking for?"

"Hey!" Joe interjected. "Don't blame the Stryx for the way you've been feeling. If anybody is at fault here, it's me. After all, it takes two to tango."

"What's with the two of you," Kelly asked suspiciously. "Somebody's up to something and I want to know what it is."

"Do you suspect a conspiracy?" Stanley asked playfully, causing Joe to groan out loud and Jeeves to make a sound like an angry paper shredder.

"That's it," Kelly exclaimed, beaming as she spotted the opportunity to remove another word from her list. "The two of you are in cahoots!"

"Damn!" Joe thumped the table and shook a fist at Stanley. "Why did you have to go and hand Dring the perfect set-up?"

"Did you put him up to it?" Jeeves demanded of Dring in his most authoritative tone.

The Maker finished inhaling a stalk of celery like a beaver knocking back a tasty reed, and gave a polite burp before replying.

"I believe that's a free month of rent I have coming, Joe. And I seem to recall something about atomic replacement bearings for my rotational mass, Jeeves." Dring reached for another stalk of celery and winked at Kelly. "And thank you, Mrs. Ambassador."

Kelly closed her eyes for a moment and reviewed the conversation. Putting it together with some nearly forgotten clues, she came to stunning conclusion.

"You three have been betting on my word list!" Kelly said in accusation. "Dring, I'm most disappointed with you, but I guess age and maturity don't always go together. And you, Jeeves. What word did you have in this silly contest?"

"Bane," Jeeves admitted. "If you could have just said that the Stryx are your bane, Dring and Joe promised to call me 'Sir Jeeves' for a year."

"And you," Kelly pointed dramatically at her husband, who was trying to hide behind an empty pitcher of beer. "Aren't you supposed to know me better than these two? What did you bet on?"

"I don't think you want me to tell you right now," Joe replied in embarrassment, and to Kelly's surprise, his ears turned pink for the first time in years.

"You spit it out, Joe McAllister," she demanded. "We're all friends here."

Joe leaned towards his wife, cupped a hand around her ear, and whispered his bet.

"Interesting contrition?" she asked skeptically. "That's not even on my list. Are you suggesting I'm supposed to be apologizing for something here?"

194

"Interesting condition," Joe repeated loudly in exasperation. "I mean, come on, Kel. You've been saying it in your sleep every night." Joe altered his voice into a bad imitation of a somnolent Kelly speaking in a British accent. "I say, isn't the ambassador in an interesting condition."

The blood drained from Kelly's face as she stared at her husband in shock. Then she looked down at her stomach and let out a little scream. "I'm pregnant?"

"You really didn't know?" Donna inquired, and burst into laughter. "You've been throwing up all over the station for weeks! We all thought you were just keeping it to yourself until the baby began to show, like the last time."

"Tinka mentioned it to me around two months ago," Chastity called helpfully from the end of the table. "The Drazen can smell the hormonal changes from a human pregnancy after just a couple of weeks."

Kelly swung her head around to check this information with Bork, who shrugged and looked a little embarrassed. "Even if I had guessed you weren't aware that you were carrying a child, I didn't think it was my place to say anything," the Drazen ambassador told her. "Just to clarify, would you like me to tell you the next time it happens?"

"I'll be forty-three next month," Kelly declared pathetically. "I thought I was just getting old. Between the stress of the Kasilian situation and the biggest auction in galactic history, I—oh, why am I even bothering to make excuses. How about you, Jeeves? Did you and Libby know all along?"

"Libby said the baby was conceived the night you, er, celebrated Aisha's arrival," Jeeves replied. "If you need the exact time of conception in order to have a horoscope drawn up by a Dollnick seer, I could check the logs for your implant."

"Yuck!" Donna said, making a face. "Am I ever glad I refused to sign that preposterous license agreement when I joined EarthCent."

"But you told me you have diplomatic implants too!" Kelly protested.

"They give them to all the employees anyway," Donna explained. "It's not worth the overhead to stock two different grades of hardware."

"Dorothy? Did you know Mommy is expecting another package from the stork?" Kelly asked her daughter.

"A baby boy," Dorothy replied. "Metoo told me."

"Metoo told you it's a boy?" Kelly asked in distress. She'd always felt that knowing the sex of a baby before it was born ruined the surprise.

"No," Dorothy answered, after furrowing her little brows in thought. "He just told me a baby, but I want a baby brother!"

Having settled the affair to her satisfaction, the seven-year-old turned back to the far more interesting conversation about grown-up boys that the young women had been conducting for the last half an hour. Paul had long since turned up the volume on his implants in defense, and was listening to the gaming news, nodding his head and saying "Yes," any time somebody looked in his direction.

"I'm beginning to think that I need a vacation," Kelly groaned, trying to remember the last time she'd been so embarrassed. When she realized how many candidates for similar humiliating experiences she had to choose from, she decided it was better to just keep talking. "When's the last time we had a real vacation, Joe?"

"Well, you took that maternity leave after you had Dorothy," Joe said.

"Did that look like a vacation to you?" Kelly demanded, then shot a guilty look at Dorothy to see if her daughter was listening.

"Your honeymoon was less than eight years ago," Donna reminded her. "Where did you go again?"

"Chez Beowulf," Kelly replied with a sigh.

"Oops, I forgot," Donna confessed with a glance at the converted ice harvester. "Still, you had Laurel then to do all the cooking. That must have been nice."

"I haven't been on vacation since I was thirty-three," Kelly continued after a moment's reflection. "I went as a volunteer on an alien archeological dig with the Open University, and we lived in oxygen tents and environmental suits. That was fun. Smelly, but fun."

"I haven't been on vacation since I was twelve," Blythe contributed from the youth table.

"Ten," Chastity added.

"What's a vacation?" the Hadad girls asked in unison, drawing a chorus of laughter.

"I haven't slept in twenty years," Jeeves contributed in a modest attempt at one-upmanship, while Kelly wondered what had possessed her to bring up the vacation subject in a room full of cheerful workaholics.

"What's sleep?" Dring asked, as he snapped a carrot in two for easier ingestion. "But then again, I don't suppose I can complain, since I haven't had a real job in almost a full galactic rotation."

"Since you brought up work, can I ask you a couple questions about the Effterii?" Clive pounced on his opportunity. "I didn't want to bore anybody, but with Kelly's interest in archeology and all, I guess it's alright."

"Libby briefed me on your quest," Dring replied easily. "It happens that I can help, or rather, we can help."

"You know where there's a Key of Eff and the Stryx will help me get it?" Clive could barely restrain his excitement.

"I know where there's a Key of Eff and the ambassador can help you get it," Dring replied. Then he turned and addressed Kelly. "I assume you still have the necklace that Yeafah pressed on you?"

"It's a key to something?" Kelly asked. She was glad to have the excuse to seek privacy for a moment to get her head back together. "I thought it was just a fancy crystal. Let me go get it."

"Does this mean you'll be leaving in the morning?" Joe asked Clive, as Kelly slowly rose from the table to head inside and find the necklace.

"I'd leave in five minutes if I didn't think it was impolite," Clive replied with barely restrained euphoria. "I can't even guess at the odds for something like this, finding an Effterii ship AND finding the key in the space of just a couple of years. It makes buying a galactic lottery ticket look like a sure bet!"

Clive's last sentence nagged at Kelly as she climbed the ramp to the ice harvester's main deck. What was it Joe had told her on their only date before getting married? If the odds were more than a hundred million to one, something just couldn't happen without outside help?

"Libby," Kelly called out as she rummaged for her jewelry box under a pile of paperbacks on her dresser. "I know that you invited Clive here so he could meet Dring and get help with this key thing, but is there something more to it?"

Kelly finally located the jewelry box, which contained the necklace from Yeafah and a few pieces of costume jewelry that looked better in the Shuk than on her person. The colors swirling in the crystal pendant almost looked like they were alive with anticipation at being reunited with the lock for the first time in countless years.

"Can you keep a secret?" Libby finally asked by way of a reply

"Of course I can keep a secret. This is exactly what I was complaining about to Jeeves earlier," Kelly replied in frustration, as she took the necklace and exited the bedroom.

"Then sit down for a minute," Libby advised, just as Kelly was passing her LoveU massaging recliner. Kelly decided that the party could wait while she treated herself to a quick pick-me-up, and settled into the LoveU with a moan. The chair embraced her gently, assessed her tension and muscular rigidity, and immediately started in with a program of Fintrian nerve stimulation and neck massage.

"I was concerned about Paul and Blythe," Libby confessed. "I've made millions of matches over the years, and while the two of them make the best of friends, they aren't well suited to be husband and wife. And it's a matter of record that no human children who attended our school and shared the same Parents Day have ever married each other."

"Why's that?" Kelly asked, in an effort to take an active enough part in the conversation to avoid passing out from pleasure as LoveU drained away her tension.

"Humans have a very strong taboo against incest, and the Stryx school operates like a foster family," Libby explained. "Blythe isn't just a business partner and a former pupil, she's my friend. I couldn't watch her waste her youth tied to Paul, just waiting for something that was never going to happen."

"And how about Paul's feelings?" Kelly asked loyally, since it didn't seem fair that Libby should be rearranging the whole galaxy just for Blythe's benefit.

"Jeeves is Paul's best friend," Libby explained. "That's why I asked him to help me find your foster son his ideal match. It's the last assignment Jeeves accepted from my dating service before resigning," Libby added sadly. "He says he's too busy with other things now, but I know he just didn't want to work for his mother anymore."

For the first time ever, Kelly sat bolt upright in her LoveU without waiting for the gentle letdown cycle.

"You and Jeeves picked out Aisha for Paul and that's why I finally got an intern?" she demanded. "Libby, how could you? That's incredibly…"

"Brilliant?" Libby interrupted helpfully. "I'm afraid Blythe saw through me the second I tried the old lift tube trick. You wouldn't believe how many matches I've made over the years with that one. She's just a little suspicious by nature."

"I think Aisha's actually a good fit for the diplomatic service," Kelly said thoughtfully, already over her initial burst of indignation. "But was it so hard to find somebody for Paul that you had to reach all the way back to Earth for her?"

"I can see you've never run a dating service," Libby scolded the ambassador. "It's not as simple as just matching up DNA samples and brain scans with personal histories and aspirations. You also need to introduce couples in the right way at the right time. Despite their professional abilities, Paul and Aisha are never going to be extroverts like Blythe and Clive. I couldn't have gotten their romance off the ground if I hadn't introduced Aisha into your home."

"Is there anything I can do to help?" Kelly inquired, as she accepted LoveU's help getting back on her feet.

"Now that you know, it would help things along if you let Clive have the necklace and suggest that he take Jeeves along to protect your interests," Libby replied. "I think it will make things easier for Blythe, and her parents would worry too much otherwise."

Kelly wondered why Blythe or her parents would be worried about Clive borrowing the necklace. She tried to figure it out as she returned to the picnic, where Dring was in his glory relating tales of the long-forgotten Effterii.

"Is this what you're looking for?" Kelly asked, handing the necklace to Clive. The former cage fighter gazed transfixed at the crystal pendant, and for a second, Kelly thought he was going to break down and cry for joy.

"I'll agree to whatever deal you say," Clive told Kelly humbly. "I just want to be the first one onboard, to be part of living history."

"I'll let you take the key if Jeeves is willing to go along with you," Kelly responded. Not comfortable with the mercantile reason Libby had supplied, she added the hastily conceived explanation, "I wouldn't want it on my head if you can't control the ship."

"I'd be honored if you came along," Clive said to Jeeves. "I know you can get more out of my ship than I can, so the whole trip would take just a few weeks."

"As long as Shaina and Brinda can spare me," Jeeves replied, with a glance down the table at his new business partners.

"Go for it," Brinda told him. "We're still working out the circuit schedule and advertising, so the first auction is at least two months away. Besides, anybody who hasn't slept in twenty years deserves a few weeks off."

"It sounds like an exciting vacation," Blythe said enviously, causing Kelly's heart to skip a beat. Next to Libby, the Prophet Nabay was a mere carnival fortuneteller.

"Come with me," Clive offered instantly. "There's plenty of room on the Caged Bird, and I'm sure Jeeves and I can rig up a magic ball on a cable to get you some weight while we're coasting."

"Let me talk it over with Chastity," Blythe replied hesitantly, which was so out of character that everybody stared in her direction. Blythe compounded their surprise by starting to blush, perhaps for the first time in her adult life.

"Don't use me as an excuse," Chastity said wickedly, enjoying the once-in-a-lifetime spectacle of her older sister's embarrassment. "I'm used to you running off and pretending to do business all the time while Tinka and I deal with the actual customers."

"Well, I'm going then," Blythe shot back, without trying to figure out how she really felt about the invitation. Like a lioness looking to reestablish dominance over her pride, she reached across the table, and snapped a few times under Paul's nose to get her former boyfriend's attention. "And there will be no marriages before I get back!"

"Yes," Paul responded mechanically, having missed the entire conversation while listening to a couple of Horten analysts break down the action at the recent Nova tournament. Even Aisha had to laugh at his answer.

"On Drazen, we have a saying that there is a lid for every pot," Bork's wife observed to Donna quietly. "It looks like this applies to humans as well."

"We have the same saying," Donna replied in a similar register, keeping the conversation private to their end of the table. "But in my daughter Blythe's case, I'm not sure if she's the lid or the pot."

Two seats to her right, Joe looked sadly at the empty pitcher. Then he swapped his glass with Kelly's nearly full one, and took a happy swallow as Beowulf looked on, impressed by the trick.

"What kind of man steals his wife's beer?" Kelly demanded

"Bad for the baby and all that," Joe replied complacently. Finally he had his revenge for the cracker crumbs in bed.

EarthCent Ambassador Series:

Date Night on Union Station

Alien Night on Union Station

High Priest on Union Station

Spy Night on Union Station

Carnival on Union Station

Wanderers on Union Station

Vacation on Union Station

Guest Night on Union Station

Word Night on Union Station

Party Night on Union Station

Coming in 2017

Review Night on Union Station

Also by the author:

Meghan's Dragon

About the Author

E. M. Foner lives in Northampton, MA with an imaginary German Shepherd who's been trained to bite bankers. The author welcomes reader comments at e_foner@yahoo.com.

Printed in Great Britain
by Amazon

48284255R00125